THE SCRAPBOOK

❦ *of* ❧

FRANKIE PRATT

a novel in pictures

CAROLINE PRESTON

ecco

An Imprint of HarperCollinsPublishers

The Scrapbook of Frankie Pratt

Chapter 1

Cornish,
New Hampshire

1920

The Girl Who Wants to Write

A Corona at last—
I've always wanted one!

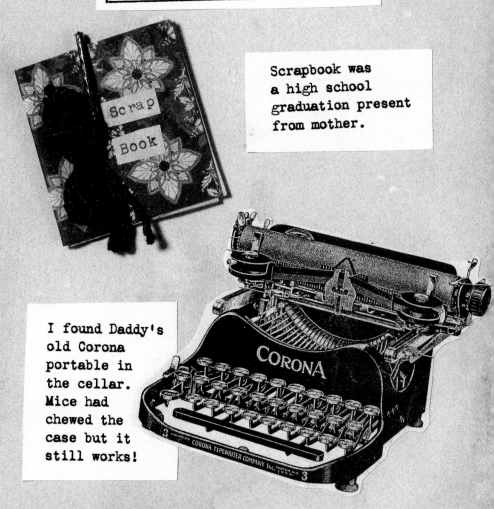

Scrapbook was
a high school
graduation present
from mother.

I found Daddy's
old Corona
portable in
the cellar.
Mice had
chewed the
case but it
still works!

Typewrite
The New Way

80 to 100 Words a Minute Guaranteed

Totally new system. Based on *Gymnastic* Finger training! Brings amazing speed—perfect accuracy—*BIG SALARIES*. Learn at home. 10 Easy Lessons. Easy for anyone. No interference with present work. **32-Page Book Free** illustrates and explains all. Gives letters from hundreds with salaries *doubled* and *trebled*. A revelation as to *speed* and *salary* possible to typists. Don't be satisfied with $8 to $15 per week. Earn $25 to $40 per week by typewriting the New Way. Write for book of proof. Postal will do, but write today—NOW!

ONLY 10
EASY
LESSONS

The Tulloss School
9870 College Hill
Springfield, Ohio.

I sent away for
a free instruction
booklet on how to
type. I will type
one page every day.

3

Nickname: "Frankie" (hate Frances!)

Birthday: Sept 5, 1902

Address: Cornish Flat, New Hampshire

Height: 5 feet 7 3/4 inches
(in stocking feet)

Weight: 116 lbs.
(in stocking feet)

Hair Color: dark strawberry blonde
with honey streaks in summer

Eye Color: blue with hazel green highlights in sunlight

Nose: straight, thin, can look
too pointy from left-hand side

Complexion: too many freckles

I have a dog
named Fritzy.

I don't have a picture that doesn't
make my nose look pointy but my
brother Teddy says this card from the
Dr. Busby game looks just like me.

BUDDY

song

C Warde Traver

Mother says I
look like this
sheet music girl.
Wishful thinking.

5

Father

Name: George Osborne Pratt

Birthday: October 18, 1872

Education: Windsor High School
   Dartmouth College, Class of 1893
   Dartmouth Medical School, Class of 1895

Teddy's cat

Bluebell

Profession: Physician, General Practitioner
         Cornish, New Hampshire

Died: January 25, 1915. Dartmouth Hospital

Daddy had a weak heart because he'd had rheumatic
fever when he was 5. (Even though his cheeks were
always pink and he had arms like a boxer.) Caught
influenza which turned to pneumonia. Died 6 days
later. They said his heart gave up. I was 12.

My parents on their honeymoon in 1900,
hiking at Smuggler's Notch. Daddy young
and handsome (always will be, never got old).
Mother still full of dreams . . .

6

Name: Roxanne Bayliss Pratt
            Nickname: Roxie

Birthday: April 24, 1878

Education:
        Windsor High School
   Licensed Practical Nurse Certificate

Mother went back to work
after Daddy died. Hired
as nurse for rich old ladies
over on Dingleton Hill.

My Brothers

Teddy & Wally

NO SISTERS

Mother, Daddy, Teddy, Wally,
and me. I am five.
Mother already getting
crease in forehead.

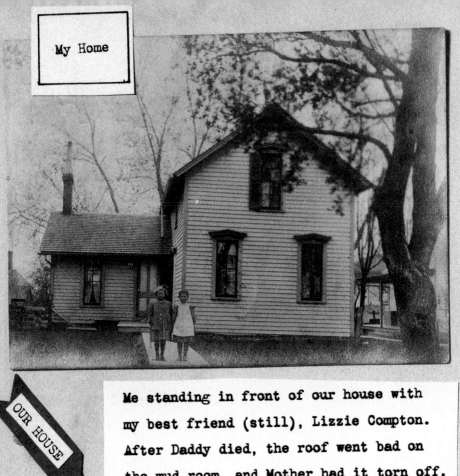

OUR HOUSE

Me standing in front of our house with my best friend (still), Lizzie Compton. After Daddy died, the roof went bad on the mud room, and Mother had it torn off.

Cornish Flat, N. H., and Croydon Mountain.

Cornish facts:
winter population: 685
summer population: 844
nearest city: Claremont

Our farmhouse still doesn't have "modern conveniences" like a gas stove or a motorized washer

And not likely to get them any time soon.
*** sigh ***

TOMATO
EARLIEST OF ALL

PRICE
10¢

BURT'S SEED FOR QUALITY

Preserve Jar Labels

5 Cents

All gummed and perforated

Can't afford to buy food at grocery store very often either. Mother keeps a big (weedy) vegetable garden and a few scraggly hens.

Tomatoes   Tomatoes

The Senior Class

invites you to be present at its

Commencement Exercises

June the twenty-sixth

at eight o'clock

I'm a High School Graduate!

HONOR
WRITING
PUPIL

Program

Music—Selected   Orchestra

Salutatio—Latine

ELSIE VIRGINIA BRAND

Oration—The Louisiana Purchase

WILLIAM WEBSTER RICE

Serenade—Abt   Double Quartette
Class Poem

Presenta...

Rece... Friends of C... Gymnasium

... COLBURN, Director ... Orchestra

Class Poem
By Frances Pratt,
Valedictorian

Success

Concentrate thy strength, O soul…
On that which most within thee lies!
Center all thy thought on that
Through which most surely thou canst rise
To heights, from whence, thine end attained,
Shall be to earth new glory gained!
Forgo and strive! Command thy soul
Forever toward some distant goal,
Some high ideal and single aim!
Nor lavish of thy strength in vain!
Achieve! Achieve! And find thy heaven
In deeds accomplished, and thy name
Among th' immortal one of Earth
Shall glorify the lists of Fame.

corsage

My valedictory poem.
Piffle but no one
seemed to notice.

Most Popular Girl: Adelaide Bullard

Most Popular Boy: Tommy Gaines

Prettiest Girl: Adelaide Bullard

Handsomest Boy: Tommy Gaines

Most Sensible Girl: Bessie Fergusen

Smartest Girl: Frankie Pratt (if I do say so myself)

Smartest Boy: Will Atwater

Tommy
most athletic
most popular
(richest)
(dumbest)

Adelaide
prettiest
most popular
(most stuck-up)

Tommy in football uniform
Will (smartest) who didn't
make the team

11

May true
friends be
around you

MY FRIENDS

Lizzie Compton
My best friend always.
Her father is postmaster.
She's the most cheerful girl
in class and can't understand
why I'm so bookish and serious.
And she CAN'T understand why
either Bessie or I would ever
want to go to college.

Bessie Fergusen
2nd best friend.
Most sensible girl in class
Is going to go to Plymouth
State to get a degree in
home economics. Can cook
and sew like a demon.

Baking Powder Biscuit

2 cups flour	2 tablespoons lard
4 teaspoons baking powder	¾ to 1 cup milk
	1 teaspoon salt

Bessie is teaching us
how to cook. My biscuits
came out like golf balls.

HUCKLEBERRY FINN

IDYLLS OF THE KING

We Play Cards

THE SCARLET LETTER

NATHANIEL HAWTHORNE

DAVID COPPERFIELD

DICKENS

I always win at Authors.
That's because all these
books are in Daddy's library.
After he died, I made a vow
to read every single one.
And I did, by the time I
turned 15.

LITTLE MEN

LOUISA MAY ALCOTT

THE TEMPEST

WILLIAM SHAKESPEARE

Now I get my books from the Cornish
library. I just finished reading Summer
by Mrs. Edith Wharton for the second
time. It's about a 16-year-old girl
stuck in a New England village.
Sounds familiar.

LEARN TO READ THE FUTURE with **OLD GYPSY FORTUNE CARDS**

We Tell Our Fortunes

My fortune.

But what does it mean. . . ?

Will Atwater (the smartest boy) asked me (the smartest girl) on an official date.

We drove to White River Junction to see Way Down East in the new picture palace. Movie was actually filmed here on the White River. Fancy that.

Afterwards, we had a big fight about Lillian Gish. Will said she is "spunky," whatever that means. I said she's insipid. The scene where she's thrown out into the snow by her fiance's mean father is just plain sappy.

Lillian Gish on a chunk of ice.

What! you never kissed a girl before? Well, you beat it, kid! You aint goin' to practice on me!

Will tried to kiss me on the lips, but I turned my head quick, so he got my cheek. Date was a complete flop!

?????????? My Future ??????????

Daddy always wanted me to go to college.
Miss Vera Jones, the principal,
arranged for me to take the Vassar
entrance exams. She was Class of 1892.
They were d-n hard, and I was sure
I flunked!

Vassar College

Dear Miss Pratt,   wants me . . .

The Vassar College Admission Committee is pleased
to inform you that you have passed the entrance
examinations and offer you a place in the Class
of 1924.

Due to Rev. Phelps's letter concerning your widowed
mother's financial situation, we are prepared to offer
you a half-scholarship. With this stipend, your tuitio
for the 1920-21 academic year is reduced to $500. In
order to preserve your scholarship, the Committee
requires that you maintain a B average.

Please accept our congratulation

Sincerely Yours,

C. Mildred Thompson

Secretary, Committee

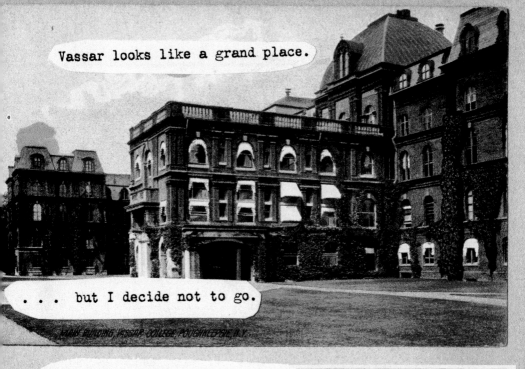

Vassar looks like a grand place.

. . . but I decide not to go.

Mother says she'll come up with the extra $500, but how? We barely scrape by as it is.

I tell Mother I don't want to go to Vassar after all. It's just a rich-girls school, I say. They'll just look down their snooty noses at a scholarship girl.

I'll get a nursing license, just like mother. Much more pratical than a degree from Vassar any day of the week.

AIN'T IT HELL TO BE BROKE

BY COURTESY OF
New York American
BY STAR CO
AMERICAN

DREAM

My first $ from Mrs. P.

I'm hired to be a nursing aid (babysitter) for 83-year-old Mrs. Pingree, one of the rich summer ladies on Dingleton Hill.

Time for the Week ending,

July 18

S	M	T	W	T	F	S	No. Days	Rate	Amount	
									Dolls.	Cts.
10	10	10	10	10	10	10	7	.25	17	50

I get paid $17.50 a week.

$10.00   to mother

$5.00   pocket money

$2.50   savings

When I've saved enough for tuition, I will start taking night courses for my nursing license.

A Day with Mrs. Pingree: a Sad Story
By Frances Pratt

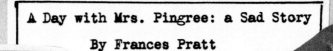

6:30 Arrive, wake Mrs. P up,
help her to the commode.
Put her glasses on.
Scrub her dentures and insert them.

7:00 Bring Mrs. P. breakfast in bed.
1 slice unbuttered toast
cup of Postum

8:00 Bring basin of warm water
and perform her "ablutions."

8:30 Brush out her wisps of white hair.

10:15 dozes off

10:30 Take breakfast tray to kitchen.
Rinse dishes.
Get bored and snoop through stuff in
pigeon-hole in library desk.
Find picture of Mrs. P
as debutante.

Mrs. P at 18

Mrs. P now

11:45 Capt. James Pingree wanders down to the kitchen, looking for breakfast. He's been staying with his grandmother since he got out of the army last year. Can't go back to his law firm in New York because lungs are scarred from mustard gas.

Captain Pingree then.

Served

2nd Artillery

Gassed at Mezy

Won Distinguished Service Medal

(Teddy's boy scout medal, which sort of looks like Captain Pingree's.)

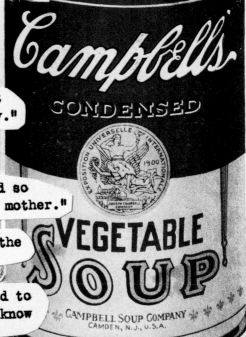

2:20 Captain heads out for his daily drive. I watch from kitchen window as he climbs in Aero roadster. He paid for it with one of Mrs. P.'s checks. He slips on tinted glasses and a tweed cap.

Checks reflection in side mirror. Vain!!

Where does he go every day? Does he have a girl?

4:30 Heat can of Campbell's soup for Mrs. P's supper.

Mrs. P. perks up for the first time all day and wants to talk.

"Your father's my doctor but he hasn't come around lately."
"He's dead."
"Since when?"
"Five years ago."
"Then you should get married so your husband can help your mother."
"I'm only 17."
"Plenty old enough. When's the Captain getting back?"
"I don't know."
"I thought you were supposed to be a smart girl. You don't know much for a smart girl."

Frankie—
Come for a drive with
me this afternoon.
I know what you'll say.....
You can't leave Gran.
But I've gotten Hobbes'
daughter Tess to come in.
I'll pack a picnic.
Won't take no for an
answer.
Meet you in the driveway
at 1:00.....
J. P.

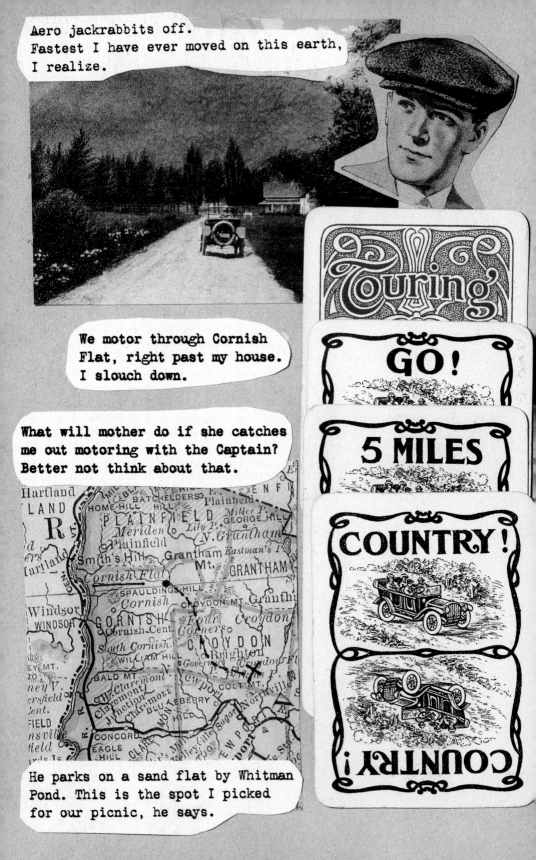

Aero jackrabbits off.
Fastest I have ever moved on this earth,
I realize.

We motor through Cornish
Flat, right past my house.
I slouch down.

What will mother do if she catches
me out motoring with the Captain?
Better not think about that.

Touring

GO!

5 MILES

COUNTRY!

He parks on a sand flat by Whitman
Pond. This is the spot I picked
for our picnic, he says.

"Sorry about the mosquitoes."
"They never bother me--I
must not taste very good."
"I find that hard to believe."
"Why is this sandwich pink?"
"Deviled ham. We ate it all
the time in the army."
"Do you think about the war much?"
"I try not to."
"That was a stupid question, I guess."
"I'd rather talk about you. So
you want to be a nurse."
"Not really."

"Well then, what do
you want to be?"
"You'll laugh."
"No I won't."
"I want to be a writer."
"What do you want to write?"
"Novels."
"Like Dickens?"
"More like Mrs. Wharton."
"But her women are
all so sad."
"So you've read
Edith Wharton?"
"Don't sound so
surprised. I wanted
to be a writer once.
A long time ago."
"Why didn't you?"

"My parents thought I should earn a living.
The war. The real answer is I don't have
much talent. Or at least not enough."

"It's still not too late. To do what you want."

"Too late for me. But not for you. It's getting hot. Do you want to go swimming?"

"I didn't bring a swim suit."

"Too bad. You could just go in your, you know, slip."

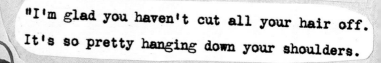

"I'm glad you haven't cut all your hair off. It's so pretty hanging down your shoulders.

Mind if I take a picture? I'm crazy about my Kodak."

"Like this?" *Snap!*

"Look up. Brush your hair back. Lovely. You're a lovely girl."

Snap!

Tomorrow at 1:00?

Let ROYSTER'S Start You on the Way to Bigger—Better Crops

ONE

MEMORANDA

SO IT'S 1:00 THEN?

1

AGAIN AT ONE

1

1:00?

DRIVING SPECTACLES.

Riding Bow.

He buys me my own pair of driving glasses.

I stop worrying if anyone in Cornish will see us.

COLLISION

HAULED IN

DELAY

What happened on August 28, 1920

This afternoon when I went to the driveway
at 1:00, there was Mother's model T, and
Jamie's roadster was nowhere in sight.
Mother climbs out, looking very grim and old.
"Where's the Captain?" I ask.
"He drove off when I pulled in," she says.
I draw a circle in the gravel with my toe.

"I don't care what you think, Mother.
Jamie and I have an understanding."

"Do you?" She sounds so sad.
"He's not the man you think
he is. I'm going to have a talk
with Mrs. Pingree."

She marches in the house and up
the stairs.
I chase along behind.

Mother goes into Mrs. Pingree's
room without knocking.

Mothers know

I stand in the hallway. Jamie's bedroom door is open. I go inside.

clipping from
Town & Country
about Jamie's wife (?!)

Corinna Pingree,
wife of war hero James Pingree,
in Lanvin at the Saratoga Races

What Mrs. Pingree Did

Mother comes out of Mrs. Pingree's bedroom fifteen minutes later and hands me a check.

$ 1000

No. 19

THE SECOND NATIONAL BANK,
OF BOSTON

Pay to the order of Frances Pratt

One thousand and —— 00/100 Dollars.

Ada Derby Pingree

Treasurer.

Dear Miss Thompson,

Is it still possible for my daughter, Frances Pratt, to be admitted into the Vassar class of 1924?

A recent change in our circumstances will allow her to accept Vassar's generous scholarship offer.

Please let me know if arrangements can be made for her to join the freshman class in September.

Sincerely yours,

Roxanne Bayliss Pratt

Vassar is still willing to take me.

Vassar College Required Clothing for Freshman Students 1920

5 white shirtwaists (with collar & modest neckline)
5 skirts (no hemlines above 8 inches from floor)
2 Vassar silk cravats ($2.50 at Campus Store)
1 pair ladies brown oxfords (2 inch heel maximum)
Freshman Beanie & Pin ($1.25; $.75 at Campus Store)
Exercise tunic and bloomers.
Corsets (no "Parisian chemises" or "Teddies")
Stockings (black or white, no "flesh tone")
Garter belts (stockings must be worn with garter belts)

Students are expected to dress modestly in the dormitories.
No men's pajamas or "shortie" nightgowns.

27K5812
All Wool Flannel
$3.98

31 R 8435
All Wool Canton Crepe
$6.98

I order my Vassar wardrobe from the Sears Catalog.

Back Lacing. For Slender and Average Figures.
18T117 $1.79

$4.65

Sizes, 2½ to 8.
Wide widths only.
Shipping wt., 1½ lbs.

15E2627
The Pair, $4.48
Dark Brown Leather
Lace Oxford—Low Heel—Medium
Round Toe—Sewed Sole.

37

Mother and the boys drive me to the train station in White River Junction before dawn on September 12.

It is already so cold we're wrapped in wool sweaters and can see our breath.

Mother hands me an envelope. Open this after you get on the train, she says.

PHILADELPHIA AND READING RAILWAY Co.

This Ticket with Coupons attached entitles the holder to ONE FIRST CLASS PASSAGE from

MONTREAL to NEW YORK, N. Y.

Good until October 31st of the Year of Issue as Stamped on Back

...ket is void unless officially stamped and dated. In sell-
...ket for passage over other lines, this Company acts only
...nd assumes no responsibility beyond its own road.
...s of baggage allowed each passenger. Company's re-
...y for baggage limited to $1 per lb. unless special agree-
...made. The coupons belonging to this ticket will be
...tached.

Gen'l Pass'r Agent.

RAILWAY EXPRESS

RAILWAY EXPRESS AGENCY

Daddy's watch chain.

Photograph of
Daddy giving me
a bottle.

The anchor charm Daddy
always wore. He said it
kept him safe.

39

I stare out the window
and watch the sun rise.
I check the roads at
every crossing.

I KNOW WHAT IT MEANS TO BE
LONESOME

NASSAU

YALE
YALE

F. EARL CHRISTY

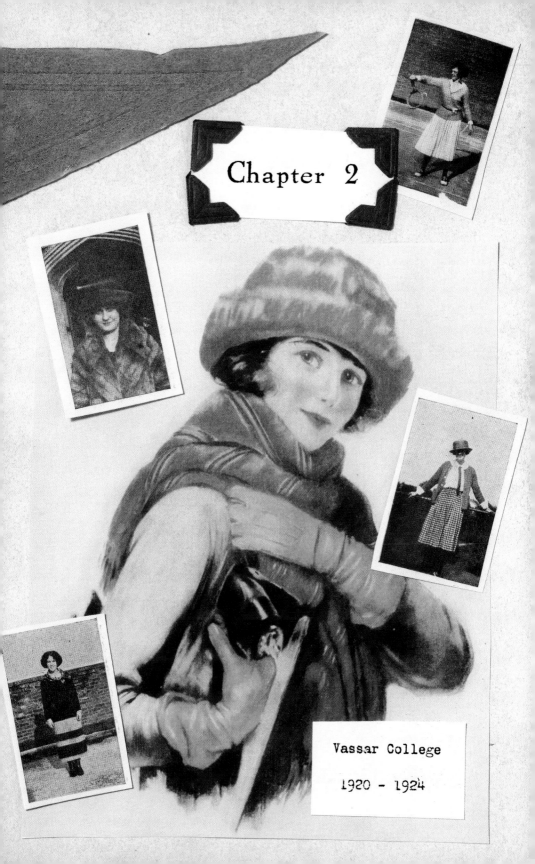

Chapter 2

Vassar College

1920 – 1924

I become a Vassar Girl

Vassar Rules

AND THE MORAL OF THAT IS:
Begin well! Remember bad work for the first year handicaps you all the way through college.

Electrical appliances are not allowed. Give your electric curling iron to your debutante sister: it will plunge the Hall in darkness if you use it here.

No matter how sick you feel when the chapel door closes in your face, a self-excuse will do you no good.

In these days of war weddings you can't tell a Miss from a Mrs. so call them all by their first names.

Campus dogs and college laundry make substantial clothes necessary.

Even though it is customary to go bareheaded on campus, Poughkeepsie is not campus.

Gym for all winter cannot be made up in a week.

Don't get a crush! It may make you famous, but you won't be liked.

Vassar Song

VASSAR GETS PUBLICITY

The girl who comes to Vassar
Must be a millionaire;
She has at least two motors,
And always dyes her hair;
To know the latest fashion
She always is the first—
In fact, she is quite dashin',
Says Willie Randolph Hearst.

Vassar Slang

Cram—To load up for exam.
Swipe—Steal—Don't do it.
Shoot him—Doing well on exam. or recitation.
Sign off—Getting leave of absence.
Bull—To orate about nothing.
To Crib—To cheat.
Shark—One who excels in classwork.
Quiz—Young examination.
Bluff—Pretending you have your lesson when you haven't.
Razorback—An appointed officer—they need licking on appointment.
Beat—To leave class if professor does not get there in ten minutes.
Cut—To stay away from a class.
Four out—Failure to make 60 on a study.
Bone—To study.

Vassar Joke

If a Vassar girl is choking,
They say she must be smoking—

CLASS SCHEDULE—First Term

HOURS	MONDAY	TUESDAY	WEDNESDAY	THURSDAY	FRIDAY
8- 9	FRESHMAN COMPOSITION				
9-10	FRENCH II				
10-11	SOLID GEOMETRY				
11-12	HISTORY of ANCIENT Greece + Rome				
12- 1	L U N C H				
2- 4	ZOOLOGY: MAN + Related mammals				
4- 6	PHYSICAL EDUCATION				HYGIENE

Pecking order of freshman girls:

1. New York City Girls
Went to Miss Chapin's.
Driven to school
by chauffeurs
who hauled in their
many monogrammed trunks.
Fathers are "in
investments."

2. Boston Girls
Went to Miss Winsor's.
Have nicknames like
Weezie and Boo.
Sunburned noses from
playing tennis.
Fathers are senators
and ambassadors.

And me, at the bottom of the heap with all
the other poor girls who went to public school.
(Even though none of us would admit being
on scholarship.)

45

Allegra

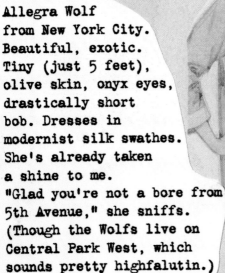

Allegra Wolf
from New York City.
Beautiful, exotic.
Tiny (just 5 feet),
olive skin, onyx eyes,
drastically short
bob. Dresses in
modernist silk swathes.
She's already taken
a shine to me.
"Glad you're not a bore from
5th Avenue," she sniffs.
(Though the Wolfs live on
Central Park West, which
sounds pretty highfalutin.)

Allegra knows EVERYTHING -- what classes to take,
how to dress, which girls we want as friends and
which ones to avoid, what clubs to join, how to
decorate our room.

46

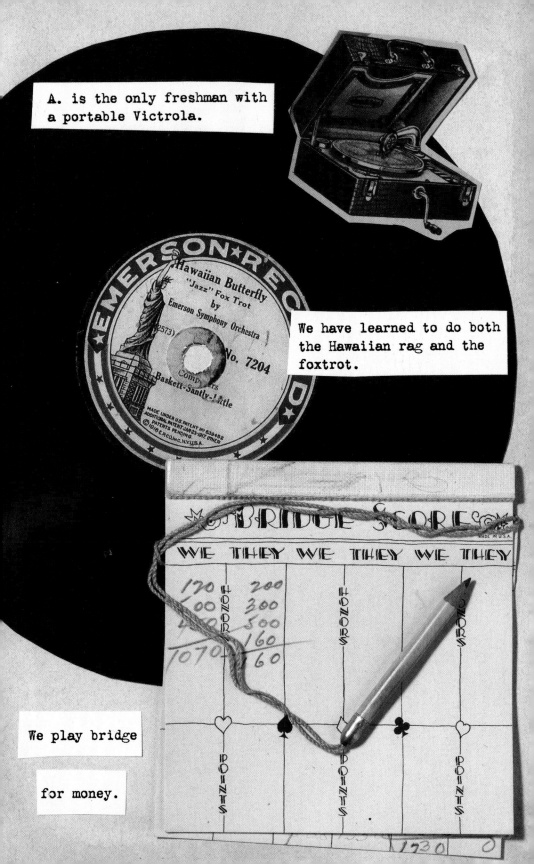

A. is the only freshman with a portable Victrola.

We have learned to do both the Hawaiian rag and the foxtrot.

We play bridge

for money.

Allegra says my long hair makes me look like a "milkmaid" and marches me to the hairdresser.

College Hair Dressing Parlors
50 Raymond Avenue, Poughkeepsie, N. Y.
Shampooing with Rain Water
Electric Scalp Treatment Manicuring Marcel Waving

(I remember how Jamie was so glad I hadn't cut my hair yet. Relieved to get it whacked off. Haven't told A. about him yet. Know she'd be sympathetic. But I don't want her to think that I'm weak or foolish. Ever.)

BOBBED HAIR PINS
MADE IN GERMANY

A. buys me some fancy European "bobby" pins.

Leona

50

Allegra Tries to Make Me Fashionable

A. says gold and platinum
are passé. The only jewelry
required is a stack of bangles
made out of some newfangled
stuff called "Bakelite."

Cashmere
Bouquet
COLGATE

Rouge the apples of your cheeks,
then a dusting of Cashmere Bouquet
powder. Finish with a swipe of
Woodbury "Passion Flower Red."

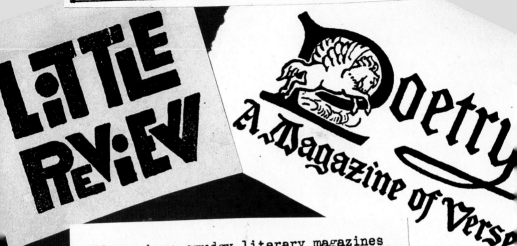

LITTLE REVIEW

Poetry
A Magazine of Verse

Allegra buys smudgy literary magazines at the Washington Square Bookstore.

She says Stein, Eliot, and Pound are the most important modern poets.

POEMS
BY
EZRA POUND.

L'ART.

Green arsenic smeared on an egg-white cloth,
Crushed strawberries! Come let us feast our eyes.

GERTRUDE STEIN

T. S. ELIOT.

The lamp said,
" Four o'clock,
" Here is the number on the door.
" Memory!
" You have the key,
" The little lamp spreads a ring on the stair,
" Mount.
" The bed is open; the toothbrush hangs on the wall,
Put your shoes at the door, sleep, prepare for life.
The last twist of the knife.

In a ribbon.
In a ribbon there is red.
Red white and blue.
Can you know why green is so is so yellow
In a ribbon for a ribbon there is a necklac
Do not say you do like beads.
I likeshells As bells.
Not as door bells.

Amazing, I say. ???????, I think.

I'm crazy about the new novel by
the Princeton boy Scott Fitzgerald.
(A. calls it "Bourgeois")

THIS SIDE OF PARADISE

I take it as a zoological
study of how rich college
boys think and talk.
(And more useful
than my zoology text,
 which I am 2 chapters
behind in already!)

By F. Scott Fitzgerald

Even though VC girls fancy themselves as "modern," their conversations about men come straight from their mothers and Jane Austen.

1. He has such a nice family.
   (filthy rich)

2. He's awfully keen.
   (going to pop the question)

3. He's not very nice.
   (tries funny stuff with girl, or not rich, or both.)

Favorite card game on the freshman hall.

OLD MAID

Forget the Dean's List! The biggest celebrity in our class is May Davenport, who announced that she's leaving VC after Christmas to get married.

What the Vassar Girl Doesn't Know About Men

Women

A ———————————————————————————————— B

C ———————————— Men ———————————— D

Diagram I

In Hygiene Class, Dr. Thelberg shows us vague diagrams and lists.

Figure 1, MALE ORGANS
FRONT VIEW

VENEREAL DISEASE

(*a*) Gonorrhea.

(*b*) Syphilis.

The Broken Joy

Mutual Adjustment

(OR)

The Glorious Unfolding

"NOTHING ESSENTIAL IS OMITTED OR LEFT IN ANY OBSCURITY."

THE SEX TECHNIQUE IN MARRIAGE

The marriage manual passed around freshman hall is even more baffling (and alarming).

CORPUS CAVERNOSUM PENIS

GLANS

CORPUS CAVERNOSUM URETHRÆ

URETHRA

D. DIAGRAM OF ERECTED ORGAN; SHOWING THE DILATION OF THE BLOOD SPACES.

POSTURES IN INTERCOURSE

1.

The Habitual Posture

2.

Posterior-lateral Posture

3.

The Astride Posture

Home for Christmas

The Myth of Winter in New England

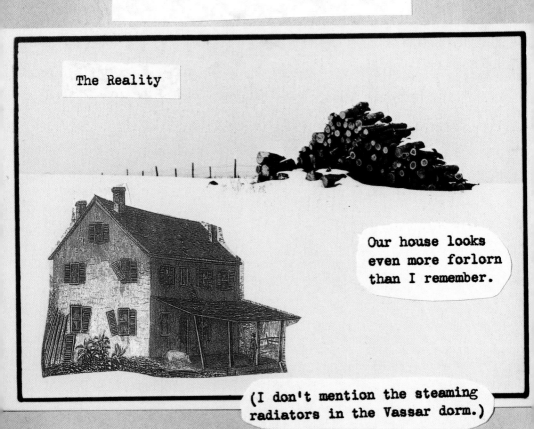

The Reality

Our house looks even more forlorn than I remember.

(I don't mention the steaming radiators in the Vassar dorm.)

MOTHER BUSBY, Dr. Busby's Wife.

Mother hunches by the kerosene lamp mending the boys' socks. She's taken on extra nursing jobs to make ends meet. I am so glad you escaped, she says to me.

MAY, 1915

Wally and Teddy save Green Stamps all fall to buy me a pen set.

PARKER

DUOFOLD

(I don't tell them I've been too busy having fun to study much, either.)

(I don't tell them about Allegra's desk drawer filled with Parker pens.)

Exit Captain Pingree

Finally, I swallow my pride

and ask Mother about Jamie.

Did he send me
a letter. . .

or try to get
in touch with me?

She looks at me hard
for a few moments.
No, she says at last.

Would Mother
lie to me?
No, I decide.
Not even to
protect me.

She says Mrs. Pingree's gone
back to Beacon Hill and the
Captain went home to his
wife in New York.

The house is closed up, and
people say the Pingrees
aren't going to come back.

One afternoon I trudge over to
the Pingrees' to see for myself.
The driveway is unplowed, and
I sink in the snow up to my knees.

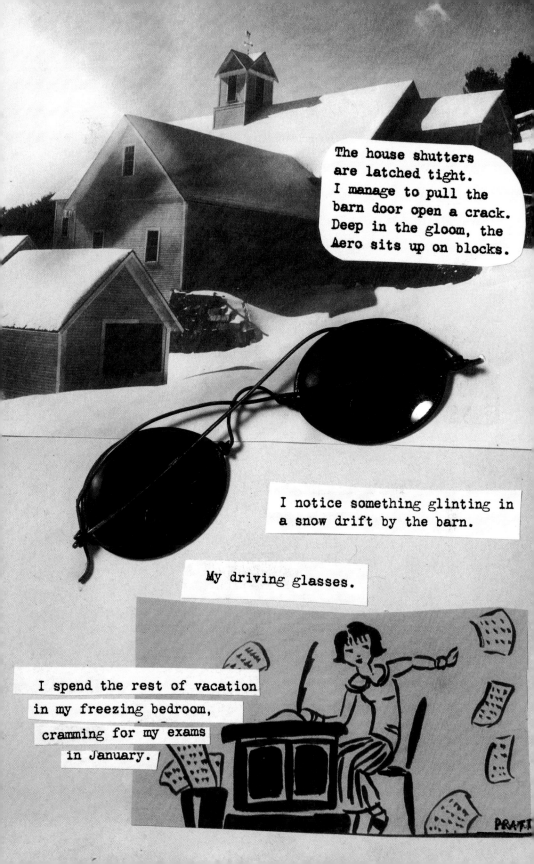

I Take My

1st Semester

Exams

The

Dismal

Results

83

Zoology

C-

Ancient History

D+

Freshman Composition

47

Se me

Solid Geometry

Failure

and last of all,
French

new pen wasn't much help, alas

PARKER

DUOFOLD

I Have a "Chat" with Dean Thompson

Am summoned to Dean Thompson's
office. Camphor smell, obese
white Persian on lap. Open file
on desk labeled "Frances Pratt."

She says:

*My professors very disappointed
in my "poor performance."
*Not surprised though,
since I wasn't as "well prepared"
as the "other" girls.
*Maybe I'm in over my head?
*Must remind me that scholarship
will be withdrawn if I don't get
grades up to B average.
(as if I'd forgotten!)
*Is Miss Wolf too "undisciplined"
and "distracting?"
*Perhaps I would do better in
a single room?

I say:

(trying hard not to snivel)
*I will apply myself and
get my marks up.
(But how?)
*I am most certainly
NOT over my head.
(I am, I am.)
*Miss Wolf is
NOT a distraction.
(She is.)
*Want to stay in my double.
(Best part about Vassar)

I Get a Tutor

Allegra finds me in the wicker chair, weeping.

"Why so glum, chum?"

I hand her my grades.

"So? Half the girls on the hall are getting C's and D's, and never crack a book."

"But I'll lose my scholarship, and have to leave school."

She looks startled. She's never considered what it means to be a poor girl without a father.

"We can't let that happen. I'll tutor you. I'm pretty good in French, and math, and writing too."

Is there anything Allegra isn't good at?

pening should be
seduction

The Theorem of Pythagoras

In a right triangle the square drawn on the side opposite the right angle will equal the squares drawn on the sides that make the right angle

repeat word to
show paralellism

insert illustrative
paragraph. should
be no single sub-points

square BC =

squares CA + AB

BLOT OUT WORRY

Verbe
Savoir
Subjonctif
Je sache
Tu saches
Elle sache

YALE UNIVERSITY, NEW HAVEN, CONN.

Allegra lends me her peach satin Patou.

How I imagine Chad Peabody. Witty and rakish, like the college boys in This Side of Paradise.

Polly Peabody invites me to the Yale Sophomore Tea Dance as the date for her brother, Chad. She says, I told him you were the prettiest girl on my floor. (I am?) He's awfully nice (that word). He's a hockey player.

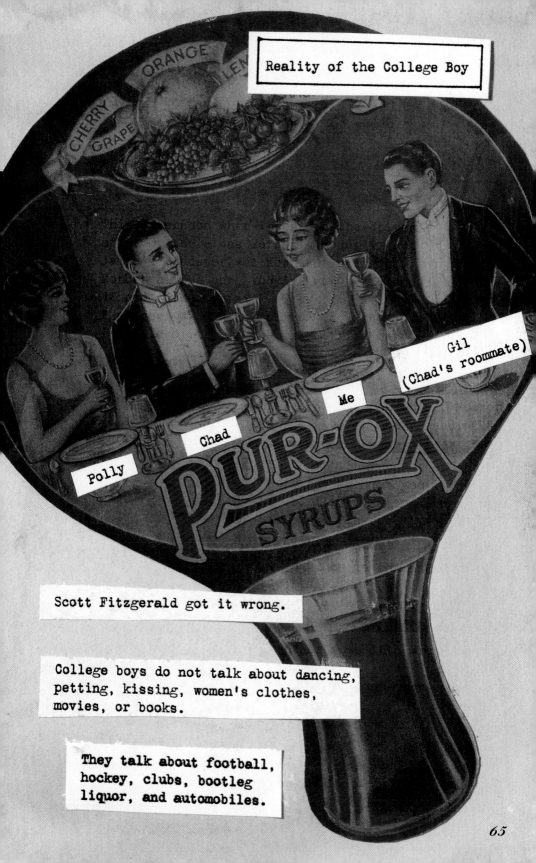

Gil
(Chad's roommate)

Me

Chad

Polly

Scott Fitzgerald got it wrong.

College boys do not talk about dancing, petting, kissing, women's clothes, movies, or books.

They talk about football, hockey, clubs, bootleg liquor, and automobiles.

65

at I Learn from Chad Peabody

'm not much of a dancer.
the colored dances.

> F. The what?

Rag, shimmy, black bottom.
e like that.

> F. So. How are you liking Yale?
> (Cringe-- stupid thing to say.)

f is rot, like Theories of the Leisure Class,
lly makes fun of being wealthy. Getting
ean says pull them up or I'm out.

> F. (Perking up) Me too! But my roommate's
> very clever and is helping me cram.

told me about your roommate. The Jewish girl.
er's in my class, you know. Oliver Wolf.

> F. (A's never mentioned a brother-- why not?
> Bet Oliver Wolf knows how to dance and
> understands Veblen. I swivel around.)
> Is he here?

not. They keep to themselves, you know.

> F. No, I don't know.

t. Maybe you should switch roommates.

I Meet the Wolfs

--I didn't know you had a brother at Yale. (me aggrieved)

--Why would you want to know about Oliver? (she shrugging)

--You're my roommate. I'm interested in your family.

--Maybe I'm embarrassed by my family.

--Maybe you're embarrassed by me. (me now teary)

--Oh, come on.
(she using a soothing voice)
If you're so interested in the Wolf family, come home with me for spring vacation. But I'm warning you. My parents are stuffed shirts and Oliver's a pest.

The Wolfs' chauffeur, Louis, picks us up in the Packard.

Mr. Wolf's library

the music room

apartment has
a second floor!!

windows look out
over Central Park

Lucie the maid.
A. speaks to
her in French.

Enter Oliver Wolf

One morning, I find a man stretched
across the living room sofa.
Oh, hello, he says, stumbling to
his stocking feet (hole in one toe),
pushing messy hair off his forehead.
"I'm Oliver. I know who you are.
The one who gave that dolt Chad
Peabody the cold shoulder."

He drinks coffee and
peppers me with questions.
Tell me about your parents,
your brothers, Cornish.
How do you like Vassar?
How are the other girls?
Who's your favorite writer?
(Fitzgerald, I say, instead of
Wharton.)
What do you want to do after
graduation? Not get married,
I hope.
(Write for a magazine, I say.)
Where do you want to live?
(New York, maybe Paris.
Not Cornish!)
And then he listens closely
to my answers, nodding as if
they were profound.

Allegra never asks me
questions, I realize.
She only makes
pronouncements.

Oliver looks like a
bedraggled Arrow Shirt man.
Moth holes in sweater,
buttons missing from coat,
spots on tie.

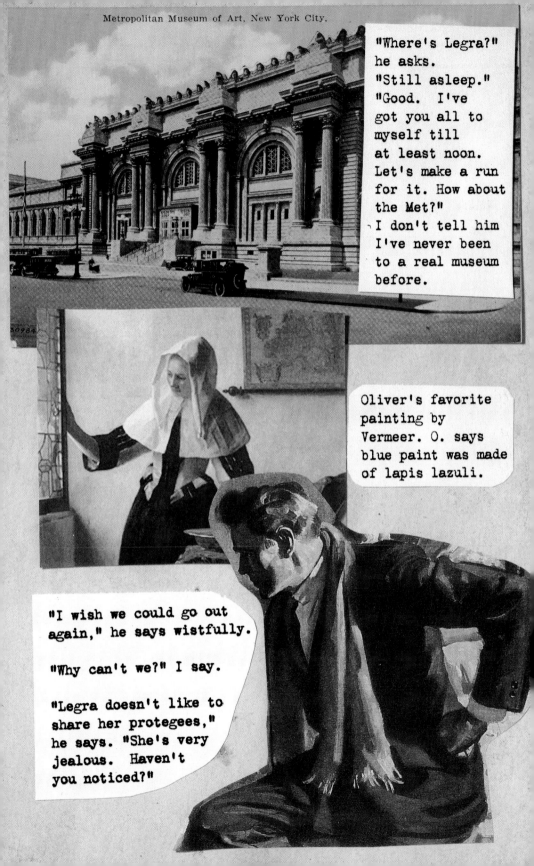

Metropolitan Museum of Art, New York City.

"Where's Legra?"
he asks.
"Still asleep."
"Good. I've
got you all to
myself till
at least noon.
Let's make a run
for it. How about
the Met?"
I don't tell him
I've never been
to a real museum
before.

Oliver's favorite
painting by
Vermeer. O. says
blue paint was made
of lapis lazuli.

"I wish we could go out
again," he says wistfully.

"Why can't we?" I say.

"Legra doesn't like to
share her protegees,"
he says. "She's very
jealous. Haven't
you noticed?"

VASSAR COLLEGE
RECORD FOR 2nd SEMESTER 1920-1921
Frances Pratt

Course	Hours	Grade
English 1		B
History 30		B-
Mathematics 2		B
Zoology 12		B-
French 2		C-
Hygiene		B
Physical Education		B

Total credits received through June, 1921

C. Mildred Thomps

(OVER)

I manage to pull most
of my grades up to
a low B.
Except French, my
"bête noire."
Dean Thompson
puts me on
academic probation.

She says I need
to spend the summer
at Vassar and be
tutored in French
by Mlle. Monnier.
If I pass a make-
up exam, I can keep
my scholarship.

I can stay
in the boarding-
house where all
the spinster
faculty live.

They give me
a job in the
library typing
catalog cards
to earn my keep.

Great Head (Highest Point on Atlantic Coast), Bar Harbor,

My Dreary Summer

My friends send me postcards from their glamourous travels.

Allegra is doing a grand tour of France.

Polly Peabody is at the Bar Harbor Club.

GREETINGS FROM
VASSAR

Dear Allegra,

    Thanks for PC's from Chartres, Versailles, Mont-St-Michel, etc. I'm v. jealous.

    I'm enduring Mlle. Monnier's endless corrections and learning the Dewey Decimal system. In the evenings, I play cribbage with Dean McCaleb. (some fun!)

    I have become great friends with Miss Sandison who says we can both take her advanced fiction writing class next year!! She gave me Women in Love by DH Lawrence, which is banned. Pretty hot stuff! Also short stories by Katherine Mansfield, my new heroine.

Don't run off with a gigolo. . .

    F.

VASSAR·COLLEGE
PURITY AND WISDOM
A.D.1861

My Star Rises

A - much improved

A nice job

Prof. Sandison tells me that my short stories show "promise." First words of praise from a Vassar teacher.

My first A's

I write book reviews for the Vassar Review sophomore year.

I'm the Book Review Editor my junior year.

THE WASTE LAND
T. S. Eliot
Reviewed by Frances Pratt, 1924

The Waste Land is a mosaic made of a thousand patterned bits, some familiar, some old, some new and personal to the their poet, making up a pattern obscure in design and seemingly lacking in unity. One comes away from the first reading confused, amused, and deeply unsettled.

A
clues to th
two book
Bough."

A LOST LADY
Willa Cather
Reviewed by Frances Pratt, 1924

Marian Forrester is the symbolic flower of the Old America West. At first, she appears to draw her strength from that solid foundation, bringing delight and beauty to her elderly husband, to the small town of Sweet Water where they live, to the prairie land itself, and to the young narrator of her story, Neil Herbert. All are bewitched by her brilliance and grace, and all are ultimately betrayed. For Marian longs for "life on any terms," and in fulfilling herself, she loses all she loved and all who loved her.

The
VASSAR
REVIEW

Senior year, Allegra and I make the masthead.

EDITOR-IN-CHIEF

ALLEGRA WOLF, 1924

ASSISTANT EDITOR

FRANCES PRATT, 1924

Valentines (lack of)

MY TINE

FOR VALEN

THINKING ABOUT YOU EVERY DAY AND YOU ARE IN MY HEART TO STAY

You wonder why I wear this cape, But if you start inspecting You'll find it's really nothing But a cloak for my affections

Valentine's Day at Vassar makes me glum. The other girls get scads of cards from beaus and fathers. And roses. And velvet boxes from Tiffany's.

Bear me in mind, my Valentine.

VALENTINE GREETINGS

Cards I found tossed in the mailroom tra

here

is

the

to

My

My senior year,
I get ONE valentine.

A handmade one, like the ones
Lizzie, Bess, and I would
send the boys in our class.

Who is my secret admirer?

I analyze the clues.

* Cornish postmark

* typed address
(because I
would recognize
handwriting?)

Conclusion:

I want to believe
it is from Jamie.

But Lizzie & Bessie
probably sent it as
a gag.

Or my brothers.

There is no great
love on my horizon.

Allegra and I both submit stories for the Addison Prize awarded to the best short story by a Vassar student.

ARGUMENT 10

A family counsel with you or about you.

Beware the sorrow you will c... some- one by what you are planning to do.

Someone is tempting the **10** one you love.

The Picnic

short story by Frances Prat

"Sorry about the mosquitoes."

"They never bother me-- I must no

"I find that hard to believe."

"What's the pink stuff in this sandwich?"

"Deviled ham. We ate it

"Do you think about the

"I try not to."

"That's a stupid ques

"I'd rather talk abo

"Not really."

"Well, what do you

"You'll laugh."

"No I won't."

Frankie, dear,
Afraid this story comes off as somewhat naive. You imply that the girl feels humil- iated and violated by the older man only because he has taken snapshots of her with his Kodak. He certain- ly would have taken her virginity as well! Remember--write what you know. Nice effort, though. Keep trying.
A.

I make the mistake of showing my submission, "The Picnic," to Allegra for a critique.

78

March 18, 1924

Dear Miss Pratt,

We are pleased to inform you that your story "The Picnic" has been awarded the 1924 Addison Prize.

Many congratulations.

Allegra's reaction to the news that I've won the Addison Prize.

The next week, Allegra announces she is moving out of our room. "Face it, Frankie. We just don't see eye to eye anymore," she says. She moves in with a sophomore named Ruth Wheatley, her newest protegee.

Vincent Comes to Vassar

Edna St. Vincent Millay, Class of 1917, Vassar's most famous and infamous grad is returning to give a poetry reading!!

Vincent won the Pulitzer Prize in 1923. The first woman ever to win.

Miss Sandison makes me Vincent's official campus escort, "because of the Addison Prize," which makes A. glower.

All the girls love the racy poems about her lovers.

My candle burns at both ends ;
It will not last the night ;
But ah, my foes, and oh, my friends—
It gives a lovely light !

Thursday

AND if I loved you Wednesday,
Well, what is that to you ?
I do not love you Thursday—
So much is true.

First
impression:
tiny inside
Persian
lamb coat,
flaming hair
hacked off
at ears,
eyes weary,
fingers yellow
from chain-
smoking.

I tell Vincent
that "Lament"
reminds me
of my mother
after
Daddy died.

I wrote that
for _my_ mother,
she says, who
was a nurse.
Vincent went
to VC on
scholarship
too.

I tell her I
plan to go home
after graduation
to help out.

Don't get
sucked back
if you want
to be
a writer,
she warns.
Make a break,
run for it.

Lament

LISTEN, children :
Your father is dead.
From his old coats
I'll make you little jackets ;
I'll make you little trousers
From his old pants.
There'll be in his pockets
Things he used to put there,
Keys and pennies
Covered with tobacco ;
Dan shall have the pennies
To save in his bank ;
Anne shall have the keys
To make a pretty noise with.
Life must go on,
And the dead be forgotten ;
Life must go on,
Though good men die ;
Anne, eat your breakfast ;
Dan, take your medicine ;
Life must go on ;
I forget just why.

Edna St. Vincent Millay

VASSAR

Class of 1924

Commencement

1924

SmithBrothers' RESTAURANT

SODA FOUNTAIN AND LUNCHEONETTE

Operated at the Home and by the Makers of S. B. COUGH DROPS

Breaded Veal Cutlet, Tomato Sauce, Potato		$1.35
Broiled Select Ham Steak, Jelly, French Fried Potatoes		1.35
Chicken a la King on Toast, Whipped Potato		1.35
Griddle Cakes and Syrup	.40 With Bacon	.65
Welsh Rarebit	.75 Golden Buck Rarebit	.90

I have the chicken a la king. Mother has the Welsh rarebit. Wally and Teddy have the griddle cakes with bacon.

PRICE, 10 CENTS

I treat the boys to tins of their famous cough drops.

Mother hands me a card with $400. It must have taken her 2 years to save so much.

Play money. Real stuff in bank.

Something to help you get started in your new life, she says.

85

85% of the 1924s say their career plans are "wife and mother"

THE RING

? THE FUTURE?

Her Post Graduate A.B.

A few serious girls plan to become doctors and social workers. One even wants to be a "union organizer."

Under "future career," I write "starving artist."

And I am on my way.

ed by CHARLES DANA
N for IPSWICH MILLS.

Future New York, "The City of Skyscrapers," New York.

Chapter 3

GRamercy 3-9304

Air-Cooled

THE OHIO MATCH CO.

"It's a Wicked Place—"

Greenwich Village

1924 - 1925

PRICE 25¢

THE

RED BOOK

Information and Guide

NEW YORK

Manhattan and The Bronx

NEW SECTIONAL MAP

TROLLEYS,
HOUSE NUMBERS
SUBWAYS, ELEVATED
ETC — ETC.

Interstate Map Co.,

239

A week after graduation, I roll into Grand Central Station, check my two suitcases and typewriter with a redcap, and buy a guidebook at the newsstand. Vincent told me Greenwich Village was the only place for an artist to live.

Copyright 1925 by
E.R. TROTT

SUBWAY EXPRESS STATIONS   SUBWAY LOCAL STATIONS   ELEVA

So how do you start to
seek your fortune?
Here is my to-do list.

1. find way around NYC
   (buy map)
2. figure out subway and buses
   (study map)
3. find place to live
   (check newspaper)
4. open bank account
5. find job
   (check newspaper)
6. write novel
7. get novel published
8. find the love of my life

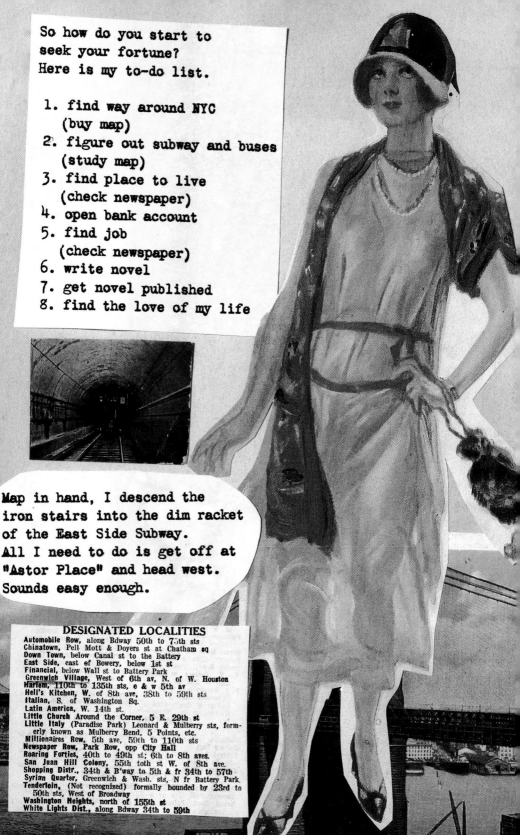

Map in hand, I descend the
iron stairs into the dim racket
of the East Side Subway.
All I need to do is get off at
"Astor Place" and head west.
Sounds easy enough.

DESIGNATED LOCALITIES

Automobile Row, along Bdway 50th to 75th sts
Chinatown, Pell Mott & Doyers st at Chatham sq
Down Town, below Canal st to the Battery
East Side, east of Bowery, below 1st st
Financial, below Wall st to Battery Park
Greenwich Village, West of 6th av, N. of W. Houston
Harlem, 110th to 135th sts, e & w 5th av
Hell's Kitchen, W. of 8th ave, 38th to 59th sts
Italian, S. of Washington Sq.
Latin America, W. 14th st.
Little Church Around the Corner, 5 E. 29th st
Little Italy (Paradise Park) Leonard & Mulberry sts, form-
   erly known as Mulberry Bend, 5 Points, etc.
Millionaires Row, 5th ave, 59th to 110th sts
Newspaper Row, Park Row, opp City Hall
Roaring Forties, 40th to 49th st; 6th to 8th aves.
San Juan Hill Colony, 55th toth st W. of 8th ave.
Shopping Distr., 34th & B'way to 5th & fr 34th to 57th
Syrian Quarter, Greenwich & Wash. sts, N fr Battery Park
Tenderloin, (Not recognized) formally bounded by 23rd to
   50th sts, West of Broadway
Washington Heights, north of 155th st
White Lights Dist., along Bdway 34th to 59th

Greenwich Village

WASHINGTON ARCH, NEW YORK CITY.

GREENWICH VILLAGE
Just west of Washington Square

The "Latin Quarter" of New York.

Home of artists, sculptors, writers, musicians, etc.

Here is where genius, temperament, smocks and flowing ties predominate—New York's Bohemia! Greenwich Village is famed for its unconventional modes of living and its gay night life.

Cellars, attics and even barns are utilized as studios, cafes, and clubs. A bizarre form of decoration, a unique adaptation of modern embellishment and a disposition to create "atmosphere" all combine in luring tens of thousands to Greenwich Village's "Pepper Pot," "Samovar," "Nut Club," "Pirates Den," and a hundred other popular rendezvous. Here at rough wooden tables with crude chairs fairly good meals are served.

Subdued light of tallow candles socketed in old beer bottles are used to emphasize the "atmospheric" environment and altho tea and "near beer" are supposed to be the popular stimulants which help in making merry at the various dining places of the district, it is whispered that every now and then the Volstead law is violated and that genuine "fire-water" can be located at certain oasis in the desert. Actual speak-easies are so cleverly camouflaged as to fool the cops assigned to the neighborhood—all of which seems to add to the attraction of the community as a whole and augment the crowds of visitors who visit the Village nightly.

COMMUNITY HOUSE
A sort of Town Hall and general community center.

I pop into the famous Pepper Pot for a cup of oolong and a crumpet. (25 cents with tip) The waitress (a careless flapper, smoking, henna hair, lipstick caked on teeth, no stockings) sees my Red Book. "Let me guess. You just finished college and you're moving to the Village to become an artist."

Is it that obvious?

"I need to find a place to stay first," I murmur. Do I sound as naive and foolish as I feel?

"Check out the bulletin board at the Washington Square Bookshop," she says. "Landlords post notices for empty apartments after the latest aspiring artist skips town owing six months rent."

THE PEPPER POT 146 WEST FOURTH ST.

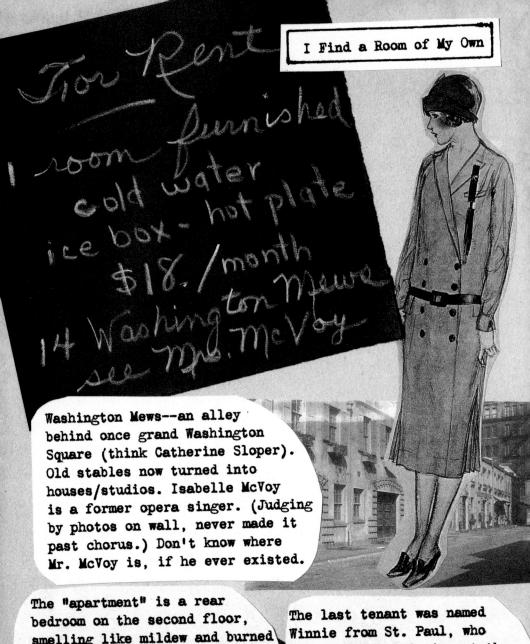

For Rent —
1 room furnished
cold water
ice box - hot plate
$18./month
14 Washington Mews
see Mrs. McVoy

Washington Mews--an alley
behind once grand Washington
Square (think Catherine Sloper).
Old stables now turned into
houses/studios. Isabelle McVoy
is a former opera singer. (Judging
by photos on wall, never made it
past chorus.) Don't know where
Mr. McVoy is, if he ever existed.

The "apartment" is a rear
bedroom on the second floor,
smelling like mildew and burned
coffee. The bathtub and toilet
are on the first floor, shared
by 3 other tenants.

The last tenant was named
Winnie from St. Paul, who
was studying painting at the
Art Students League. She left
a dragon kimono, a tube of
Tangee lipstick, and nude
sketches of herself in
suggestive poses.
"Typical," sniffs Mrs. McVoy.

VOG **McCALL'S**

I Search (in Vain) for a Job

I apply for a job at every magazine office I can find in Manhattan. No one seems impressed that I was the assistant editor of the <u>Vassar Review</u> or that I won the Addison Prize.

They all ask if I can type, but the Vassar degree is a liability. They seem to think any Vassar girl is too uppity to be a mere typist. That she'd actually try to EDIT or WRITE something herself.

Collier's

Liberty

A Weekly for Everybody

Woman's Compa

VANITY

THE SATURDAY EVENING POST

The editor at <u>Time</u>
says if I'd gone to
Yale (meaning if I were
a man), he'd give me a
try. He means this as
a compliment.

<u>Vanity Fair</u> offers me a
job as a reporter for
their Society page, then
withdraws the offer when
they learn I expect
to be paid. Apparently,
a Vassar girl should
consider it a privilege
to work for free.

Harper's Bazar

TIME

ome
nion

FAIR

The most congenial spot for the unemployed is the Automat in Times Square. Search the want ads, read a novel, scribble on a story without any dirty looks from a waitress. Sit undisturbed from 8 until 6—like going to an office. All that's required is spending a nickel every few hours on a bowl of oatmeal, an egg salad sandwich, a slice of pie (lemon meringue highly recommended), and yet another cup of coffee.

The AUTOMAT - as famous as the New York Skyline

Unemployed at the Automat

AUTOMAT

HORN & HARDART

TIMES SQUARE - NEW YORK

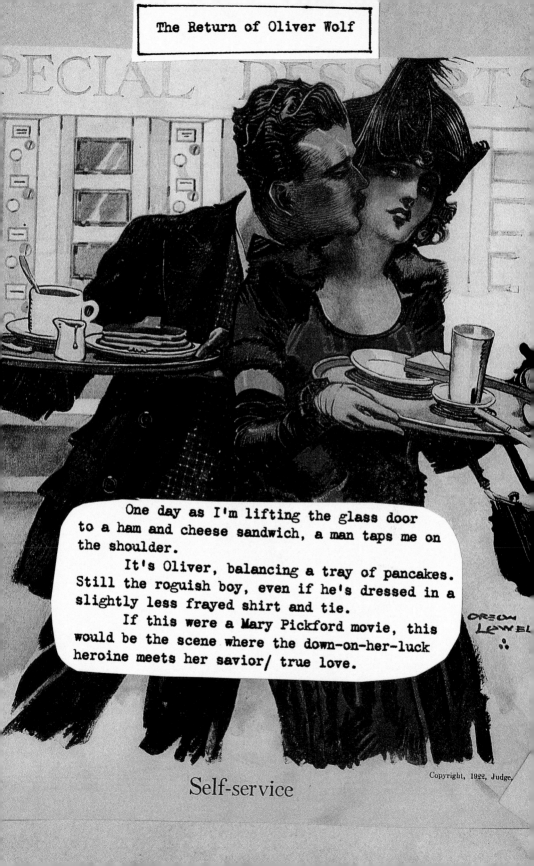

The Return of Oliver Wolf

One day as I'm lifting the glass door to a ham and cheese sandwich, a man taps me on the shoulder.

It's Oliver, balancing a tray of pancakes. Still the roguish boy, even if he's dressed in a slightly less frayed shirt and tie.

If this were a Mary Pickford movie, this would be the scene where the down-on-her-luck heroine meets her savior/ true love.

Self-service

He pulls up a chair at my table.

"Slumming it?" I say.

"Nope. I'm a bona fide member of the proletariat on my lunch break."

"You have a job? Doing what?" It's hard to imagine the rarefied Wolfs doing anything so ordinary as working for a living.

"Staff writer for a magazine."

"Which one?" It figures that feckless Oliver would have an easier time than me.

"It's a new magazine so it doesn't have a name yet. But all the great writers from Vanity Fair and Judge have come over."

"Could they use a distinguished Vassar grad?" I ask, trying not to sound desperate.

"Sure. . ." he trails off. "Except no one's getting paid yet."

"I'm afraid I need to earn my keep."

"We should go to the movies sometime," he says.

"I thought you weren't allowed to be friends with me."

"Now that you're on the outs with Legra, I'm allowed. Besides, I've moved out so I hardly ever see her. I have a room in a very seedy hotel in Chelsea."

"As I said, slumming it. What's she up to these days?" I dread asking.

"She's going to graduate school at Columbia. She's determined to have Vassar fire that writing teacher and hire her instead."

"You've got to hand it to Allegra. She knows how to carry a grudge."

"That's your third piece
piece of cake," I say.

"I was never
allowed to come
to a place like
this when I was
a kid. Too many
germs my nurse
said. So I'm
overcompensat-
ing. That's
what my psychi-
atrist says."

"I didn't know the
proletariat saw
psychiatrists."

"I'm full of contra-
dictions. I steal
things, too.
Have a spoon."

"Thanks. I'll hide
it in my purse."

HOW AN AUTOMAT WORKS

FIRST
DROP YOUR
NICKELS
IN THE SLOT

THEN TURN
THE KNOB
THE
GLASS DOOR
CLICKS OPEN

LIFT
THE DOOR
AND, HELP
YOURSELF

HOPN & HARDART

"This is where
you should work,"
he says, pointing
at a want ad.

"True Story?"

"Don't knock it.
Most popular
magazine in
America. Pays
30 bucks a week.
And think of all
those sob stories.
Great material
for a novel."

"So, how about that movie?"

"All right. Why not?"

True Sto

*Truth Is
Stranger
Than
Fiction*

I Find a Job!!

The next day, I go over to the Macfadden publishing empire at 1926 Broadway to apply for a job as staff writer at <u>True Story</u>.

I give my application to the secretary and, after an hour wait, she says, "Mr. Macfadden will see you now." The great man wants to meet me?

June
A MACFADDEN 25 CENTS PUBLICATION

Bernarr Macfadden--famous health and physical fitness crackpot and publishing tycoon. Has written dozens of advice books on how to prevent everything from dandruff to sexual frigidity.

An elevator whisks me up to the top-floor office filled with framed covers of True Detective, Physical Culture, True Romance, and Movie Magazine.

Macfadden pops out of a back room like the Wizard of Oz, dressed in a natty windowpane plaid suit. (Thank goodness he's not flexing half-naked like he is in his ads!)

"So, Miss Pratt, what makes a Vassar girl think she's qualified to tell the stories of real people who have actually suffered?

My New Boss, Bernarr Macfadden

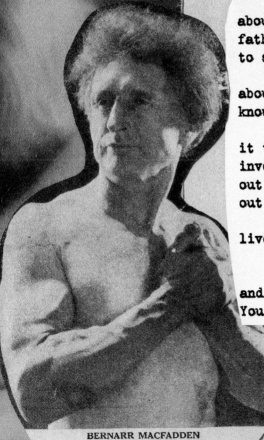

BERNARR MACFADDEN
As he is today, age fifty-eight. This photograph was taken a short time previous to the appearance of this advertisement

"I think I know something about sorrow, Mr. Macfadden. My father died young, leaving my mother to support 3 children."

"Most of our stories are about heartache. What do you know about that?"

I pause-- just say whatever it takes to get the job. "I was involved with a man who turned out to be married." Straight out of True Story!

He looks pleased. "But you lived to regret it?"

"Yes, sir, I did."

"Atta girl. Sin, suffer and repent. That's our motto. You're hired."

He turns to a shelf of Bernarr Macfadden books and pulls out "Womanhood and Marriage." "You may find this useful, Miss Pratt. Let me know if you have any questions."

50,000.00 in Cash
for TRUE STORIES
Your Own Story May Be Your Fortune!

THE publishers of TRUE STORY Magazine ar[e] going to pay $50,000 to three hundred ar[e] eleven men and women in amounts rangi[ng] [fr]om $5,000 to $100 in exchange for true stories. Why not be among them?

Never was such an offer made before. Never before did men and women who are not professional writers have such a glorious opportunity to turn their life experiences into handsome sums of money.

Nearly every man and woman has lived at least one story which, because of its unassailable truth, because it is actually a part of the life, the sorrows, joys, experiences of a fellow human being, has more power for good, more power to thrill and charm and hold the reader than any fiction story ever written.

indefinitely upon the [...] humanly possible to raise the qua[...] [...]RY to an even hig[h] [...] desire and in [...] in order to [...]gnantly i[...] [...]ghly he[...] [...]e do [...]erien[...]

RULES **TRUE S[TORY]**

All stories [...] Typewritte[n] manuscripts [...] cepted. Per[...] Write on [...] use thin ti[...] full name [...] of first p[...] pages. Addres[s] Contest [...] Unless s[...] in the co[...] Enclo[se] envelop[e] Ever[y] manus[...] sible f[...] to ret[...] Up[on] [...]dm[...]

TRUE STORY

The next day, I'm shown to my "office," a pebbled glass cubicle with a metal desk and 3 crates on the floor heaped with letters.

These are the entries for the "True Story" contest. The best sob story wins $5000 and the honor of being published in our magazine.

My job is to plow through, pick out the most "gripping" ones and then "edit" them.

THE LATEST DIRT

Dear Mr. Macfa...

This is my True ... was 16 it was a very ... good figure and a peppy personality but it was wild and didn't listen to anyone which I regret not wait even my mother wich it regret because now she is dead.

a serious boy who was in dentist school at State was intrested in me but it didn't give him the time of day. Instaid, I fell for an older man who sold Buicks. Now I am sorry.

How to edit a "true story"
1. make humdrum characters glamorous (medical instead of dental student, fashion model instead of high school junior, jazz musician instead of car salesman)
2. add dramatic plot twist (musician killed in speakeasy brawl, pronounced dead by hero who is now famous doctor)
3. finish with improbable happy ending (doctor never stopped loving still beautiful heroine)

Trapped by My Past

Knickerbocker

Entire Week
June 29th

"There's No Place as Cool as the Knickerbocker"

"I WANT MY MAN

We see I Want My <u>Man</u> at the Knickerbocker with refrigerated air. (Best thing about movie!)

20¢

GLOBE TICKET COMPANY, PHILA.

my

a lone sweeth

LYRIC

LYRIC THEA

TO-DAY
Chaplin
OF HIS GREATEST COMEDIES

Charlie Chaplin at the Lyric.

I Go to the Movies with Oliver

MAUDE MARTIN ELLIS

D ROW | CENTER | 113 SEAT
BALCONY
LYRIC THEATF

RIALTO THEATRE Program

ase
nr. Cupid—

ant
an'

ROXY THEATRE. World's largest theatre; seats over 6,200; largest permanent symphony orchestra; colossal pipe organ; played by three organists; cathedral chime of 21 bells; permanent choral group; permanent ballet corps and precision dancers, the Roxyettes; foyers and lobbies of unusual size and splendor; decorations of marvelous beauty. Magnificent stage shows. Finest talking pictures. News of the world in Fox Movietone. Refreshingly cooled in summer. Unique features of service, comfort and convenience. One of the famous show places of New York City and attended by visitors from all over the world.

Mary Astor and John Barrymore in Beau Brummel at the Rialto. The two most famous profiles in the world.

Our favorite is the new Roxy "picture palace."

ROXY THEATRE · NEW YORK CITY

ous Statue of Liberty in New York Harbor.

Things I Do with Oliver

4460. B—HIPPOPOTAMUS "PETE"
NEW YORK ZOOLOGICAL PARK

Baby Ruths
at Bronx Zoo.

Popsicles on ferry
to Statue of Liberty

POPSICLE PATENTED

(Foods forbidden by
the Wolfs, of course.)

Pell Street,

DELMONICO

CHINESE

SAVOY

CURTISS Baby Ruth America's Favorite Candy 5¢

Otto Schnering
PRESIDENT

Chop suey and egg
rolls in Chinatown.

YANKEE STADIUM
NEW YORK CITY

GEORGE HERMAN
(BABE) RUTH

BIG LEAGUE CHEWING GUM

We go to Yankee Stadium
to see the great Babe.
Hardly looks like
the world's finest
athlete-- portly, red-
faced, panting after
he runs to first.
We are busy buying
Cracker Jack when he
finally hits a home
run!

Oliver makes
me a bracelet
with Cracker
Jack prizes.

HOT
and
FREE

Cracker Jack ®

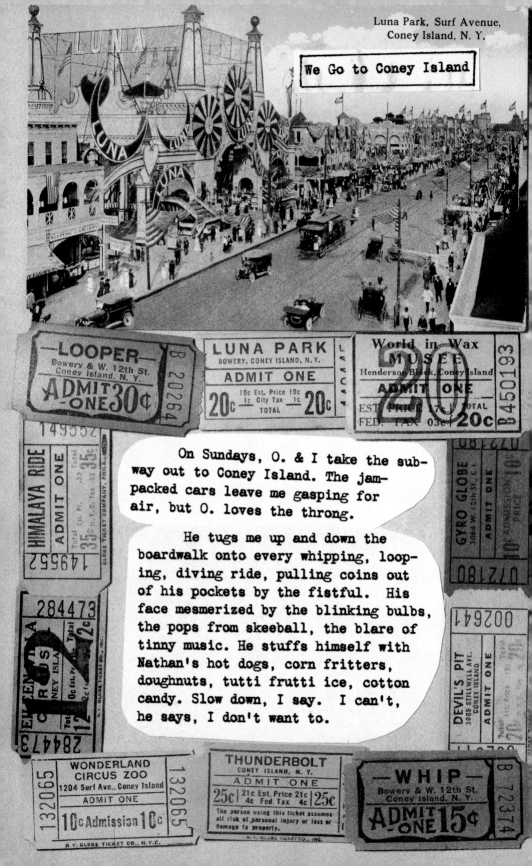

We Go to Coney Island

—LOOPER—
Bowery & W. 12th St.
Coney Island, N. Y.
ADMIT ONE 30¢
B 20264

LUNA PARK
BOWERY, CONEY ISLAND, N. Y.
ADMIT ONE
19c Est. Price 19c
1c City Tax 1c
TOTAL
20c 20c

World in Wax
MUSEE
Henderson Block, Coney Island
ADMIT ONE
EST. PRICE 7. TOTAL
FED. TAX 03c 20c
A50163
20

HIMALAYA RIDE
ADMIT ONE
Total .33
35c Est. Pr.
2c N.Y.C. Tax 02
GLOBE TICKET COMPANY, PHILA.
149552
149552

GYRO GLOBE
3064 W. 12th St. C.I.
ADMIT ONE
072180
072180

On Sundays, O. & I take the subway out to Coney Island. The jam-
packed cars leave me gasping for
air, but O. loves the throng.

He tugs me up and down the
boardwalk onto every whipping, loop-
ing, diving ride, pulling coins out
of his pockets by the fistful. His
face mesmerized by the blinking bulbs,
the pops from skeeball, the blare of
tinny music. He stuffs himself with
Nathan's hot dogs, corn fritters,
doughnuts, tutti frutti ice, cotton
candy. Slow down, I say. I can't,
he says, I don't want to.

284473
EL CENTRA
CIRCUS
NEY ISLA
Tot. 12c
0c Est. Pr. 10c
2c tax
284473

DEVIL'S PIT
3005 Stillwell Ave.
CONEY ISLAND
ADMIT ONE
002641

WONDERLAND
CIRCUS ZOO
1204 Surf Ave., Coney Island
ADMIT ONE
10¢ Admission 10¢
N. Y. GLOBE TICKET CO., N.Y.C.
132065
132065

THUNDERBOLT
CONEY ISLAND, N. Y.
ADMIT ONE
25¢ 21c Est. Price 21c 25¢
4c Fed. Tax 4c
The person using this ticket assumes
all risk of personal injury or loss of
property.
N. Y. GLOBE TICKET CO., INC.

—WHIP—
Bowery & W. 12th St.
Coney Island, N. Y.
ADMIT ONE 15¢
B 72374

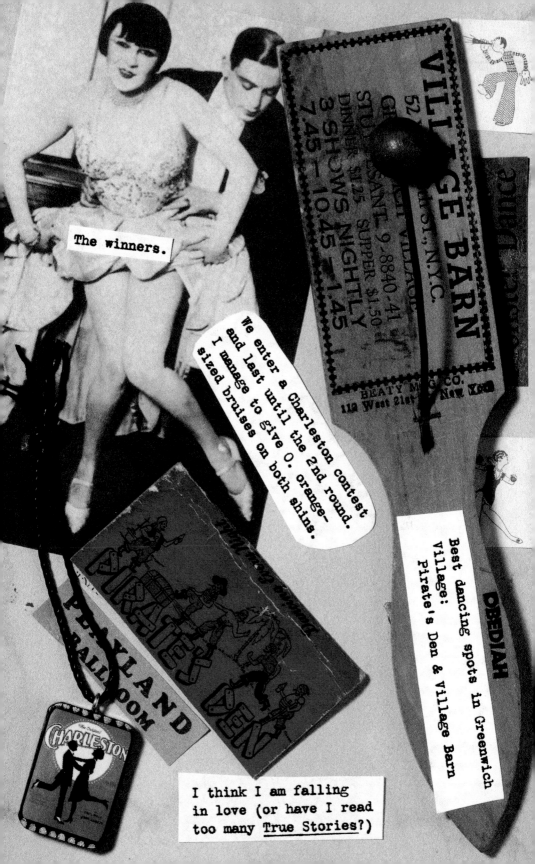

The winners.

VILLAGE BARN

52 W. 8th St., N.Y.C.
GREENWICH VILLAGE
STU[YVE]SANT 9-8840-41
DINNER $1.25   SUPPER $1.50
3 SHOWS NIGHTLY
7.45 - 10.45 - 1.45

BEATY MFG. CO.
112 West 21st St., New York

We enter a Charleston contest
and last until the 2nd round.
I manage to give O. orange-
sized bruises on both shins.

OBEDIAH

Best dancing spots in Greenwich
Village:
Pirate's Den & Village Barn

PIRATE'S DEN

PLAYLAND BALLROOM

The Original CHARLESTON

I think I am falling
in love (or have I read
too many True Stories?)

The New Yorker boasts that it will have a brand new style of cartoons. But what could be more ho-hum than a flapper cartoon?

Ethel Plummer

UNCLE: *Poor girls, so few get their wages!*
FLAPPER: *So few get their sin, darn it!*

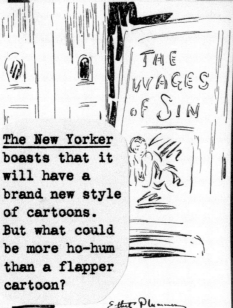

THE NEW YORKER asks consideration for its first number. It recognizes certain shortcomings and realizes that it is impossible for a magazine fully to establish its character in one number. At the same time it feels a great deal of pride in many of its features and heart-felt gratitude for the support it already has received.

THE NEW YORKER starts with a declaration of serious purpose but with a concomitant declaration that it will not be too serious in executing it. It hopes to reflect metropolitan life, to keep up with events and affairs of the day, to be gay, humorous, satirical but to be more than a jester.

It will publish facts that it will have to go behind the scenes to get, but it will not deal in scandal for the sake of scandal nor sensation for the sake of sensation. It will try conscientiously to keep its readers informed of what is going on in the fields in which they are most interested. It has announced that it is not edited for the old lady in Dubuque. By this it means that it is not of that group of publications engaged in tapping the Great Buying Power of the North American steppe region by trading mirrors and colored beads in the form of our best brands of hokum.

The New Yorker

Why the first issue is (in my humble opinion) a bore:
1. British fop on cover
2. self-important editorial
3. no color pictures
4. no table of contents
5. no author bylines

GOINGS ON

Mr. Ross calls O. "Wolf" and only lets him write the theatre and art listings in the "Goings On" section. Mostly he sends him on errands to fetch cigarettes and hooch from the bootlegger.

I don't tell O. that I think <u>The New Yorker</u> will fold in a month. <u>Poor Wolf</u> -- he had such high hopes!

Via S. S. Mauretania

Read the Truth

Dear Frankie,

I was at the Café Select yesterday (a
favorite hang out for American expats) drinking
a café au lait and struggling miserably through
Pere Goriot (for my $%&* French literature
class at the Sorbonne).
A man settled into the table next to mine
and ordered a brandy (even though it was only
11 in the morning). Mid 30s I'd guess, dark and
very handsome in a going-to-seed kind of way.
"American?" he asked. (How does
everyone always know?)
We struck up a desultory conversation and
he seemed completely bored until I said I'd just
graduated from Vassar.
"You didn't by any chance know a girl named
Frankie Pratt?" He kept his eyes on the pavement,
very nonchalant, but I could tell it was an act.
"Frankie! She's one of my best friends." I
told him you'd been the star of my class and won
the writing prize. (No surprise there, the
mystery man said.) That you were living in
Greenwich Village and writing for a magazine.
I asked him if he wanted your address.
"No. I promised I wouldn't contact her."
(What the h-e-l-l does that mean??) "But
next time you write her, please tell her that
James Pingree sends his regards."
So there you are. Message delivered.
Sometime you'll have to tell me the whole
story!
Chad's in New York too. I told him to
ask you out for dinner some time. . .

Love,
Polly

Jamie hasn't forgotten me after all.

But have I forgotten him?

My First Radio

On my birthday, O. comes staggering up to my room with a huge crate.
I pry open the top and blow away the excelsior.
It's a Radiola! It runs on batteries & is totally portable.
It only weighs 39 pounds.

We turn the dial to Hungarian Rhapsody played by Paderewski live from Carnegie Hall. So scratchy and distant, it sounds like it's broadcast from the moon.

Girls with radios have sex appeal!

F98524

Rx

Oliver Teaches Me How to Drink

KIND OF LIQUOR   QUANTITY   DIRECTIONS

DATE PRESCRIBED

THE NEW YORKER

THE LIQUOR MARKET: Sharp rise in genuine whiskies and wines due to tightening along Canadian border. Scotches: Grand Old Parr, $100@$105; King George the 4th Top Notch Scotch, $105@$110. Champagnes: Mumms Cordon Rouge, 1911, $140@$150; Pol Roget, 1919, $140@$150. Bacardi Rum, brandies and Sloe gins available at $125. Canadian Liquor Commission alcohol, per gallon, $30, supply short; Montreal flooded with low-grade alcohol imported from New York for illegal manufacture.—THE NEW YORKERS

Oliver's psychiatrist prescribes gin for his "nerves."

PRESCRIBERS PERMIT NUMBER

CITY   STATE

PERMIT NUM

STRIP STAMP NUMBE

47

O. is writing the "Liquor Market" column in the "Talk of the Town" —which he considers a great honor. Every week, he runs around town and interviews a dozen bootleggers. They give him free samples, and he has set up a fully stocked bar in my bottom bureau drawer.

CHAMPAGNE BRUT

← OLIVER   ME →

ICE
SPARKLING · CRYSTAL CLEAR

O.'s favorite drink is a "dry" martini or bourbon on the "rocks." (He smashes a bag of ice on the fire escape with a hammer.)

DRY GIN

Blended Whiskey

SINCE 1875

HEUBLEIN
VERMOUTH
EXTRA DRY

ORANGE Crush

The only way I can stomach gin is mixed with Orange Crush, which O. thinks is hilariously gauche.

After a couple of martinis, O. gets very romantic. He puts on "Rhapsody in Blue" and pulls me onto his lap. He runs a finger down my cheek and gives me long, deep kisses that make me giddy. "I love you," he says, "more than anyone in the world."

24 5 GRAIN
Spartan
BRAND
REG. U. S. PAT. OFF.
PURE
ASPIRIN
TABLETS
15 ¢ PACKAGE

"Thank you," I say stupidly, wondering what he really means.

For hangover: Take 2 Spartans with quinine water at bedtime, and 2 with Listerine before breakfast.

Womanhood and Marriage"

By Bernarr Macfadden

Don't Make the Mistake of Choosing the Wrong Life Partner!

By Bernarr Macfadden

Fill out this easy checklist to ascertain whether your suitor is a compatible match.

I. Judging A Man's Fitness

- **Y** Is he of equal intelligence?
- **Y** Is he physically attractive?
- **N** Does he have robust physical fitness?
- **N** Does he have sound mental fitness?
- **N** Is he ambitious?
- **N** Is he a good provider?
- **N** Is he responsible about money?
- **N** Does not drink alcohol to excess?

II. Are You Compatible?

- **Y** Do you have common interests?
- **Y** Do you enjoy his company?
- **Y** Are you physically attracted to him?
- **Y** Is he usually agreeable?
- **N** Do you have the same friends?

III. Do You Have Shared Values?

- **N** Do you get along with his family?
- **N** Are you the same religion?
- **?** Does he believe in matrimony?
- **?** Does he want children?
- **?** Would he be a good father?

6 # Yes

12 + He is a fine match!
8 + He is a fair match.
7 - He is completely unsuitable!

Finally, in desperation, I turn to Mr. Macfadden's book for romantic advice, and fill out this checklist.

BACHELOR 7

Trust, but not blindly.

An engagement will be broken because of you.

A new acquaintance is trustworthy.

Maybe Oliver is just a confirmed bachelor.

Oh, dear . . .

We Go to a Party

BERGDORF GOODMAN
616 FIFTH AVENUE
NEW YORK

Alden Fisher, O.'s roommate at Yale, invites us to a black tie house warming for his penthouse in a brand new building on Sutton Place.

Can't go, I sigh. Nothing to wear.

Next day, Oliver presents me with a dress box from Bergdorf's. Nestled in lavender tissue, a Premet gown in the latest color, "Acid."

We look like the haughty couple from the Arrow Shirt ad.

Neet

Neet

A fragrant antiseptic cream that removes hair

MADE IN THE U.S.A.

I use Neet to make myself downy smooth!

HIS QUICK EYE SAW THE SOFT WHITE BEAUTY OF HER UNDERARM

According to Oliver, Alden's job is sinking his family's money into "little plays no one understands."

Alden's apartment is a black & white creation by the "interior decorator" Elsie de Wolfe.

The women look sleek and bored. Suddenly, my Premet seems quite drab.

Infamous flapper Ellin Mackay, who shocked high society by running off with (older, divorced, Jewish) Irving Berlin.

I grab an "acid"-colored cocktail from a chrome tray. (No Orange Crush here.)

A Spin Around the Dance Floor

A hand grasps my upper arm and steers me towards the rubber dance floor (rolled over the parquet to prevent scuff marks . . . It's Chad Peabody.

"Well, now. You've spruced up not a dowdy Vassar girl anymor

"I guess that's a complime What are you doing these You look prosperous." (Co word for getting stout.)

"Selling stocks. Making a bu of course, like everyone els Just bought my own penthouse Madison. Bigger than this o

"Sounds impressive. Congratulat

"Thanks." (Sarcasm flying over thick head.) "Let me take you to dinner sometime."

"I'm not really very availab

"Oh, right. You engage

"Almost."

"Anyone I know?"

"Yes, actually. Oliver Wol

(A perplexed pause.) "I'm surprised. He doesn't seem like your type."

"Oh, really? What is my type?"

(A shrug.) "I dunno. Probably said enough. I need another cocktail."

Where's Oliver? I think. He shouldn't abandon me to the likes of Chad Peabody.

I wander down a long hallway, open doors, peek inside. I find him in the butler's pantry.

Kissing

Alden Fisher

on the lips.

A two to one favorite

A Fight with Oliver

Please. Please stop crying.
Why are you so upset?

Because of Alden?

I do love you.

Well, not love exactly.
It's something else.

I have feelings for
all kinds of people.

Is that all you want? I'll marry
you. We could go to a justice of
the peace tomorrow.

SLOW

Let's go back to your room and have a
drink. That will make us both feel better.

Time

To

Drop

The

Blind

Fold

The Facts

1. Oliver does love me, but it's love without passion. (Could only kiss me when he was drunk!)

2. At heart, I'm just like all those Vassar girls who only want rings on their fingers.

3. I say I want to be a writer, but all I've done so far is write True Stories.

4. It's time for a drastic change!

The next day I hand in my resignation to Mr. Macfadden.

"So, you're engaged," he says, looking pleased--his guide to marriage must have worked!

"No," I say. "I'm going to Paris." I leave before he can ask "What are you going to do there?" or "How will you support yourself?" Questions I have no answer for. . .

When I tell Oliver I'm moving to Paris, he looks relieved. No more pretending.

The CUNARD CATALOGUE
of Routes & Rates to Europe

THE WORLD'S FASTEST SERVICE DE LUXE

AQUITANIA   BERENGARIA   MAURETANIA

Weekly from New York to Cherbourg and Southampton

First Class $255 up   Second Class $147.50 up   Third Class $90 up

MAURETANIA

I take the $567.93 out of my savings account. I buy a one-way 3rd class ticket to France on the grandest Cunard ship of all, the Mauretania.

CUNARD
and ANCHOR Lines
25 Broadway   New York
or Branches and Agencies

And I bid NYC & Oliver au revoir.

Chapter 4

MAURETANIA

CUNARD
LINE

The Atlantic

January, 1926

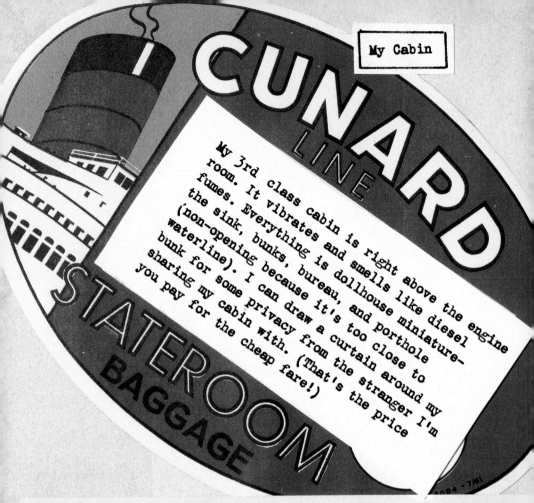

CUNARD LINE
STATEROOM
BAGGAGE

My 3rd class cabin is right above the engine room. It vibrates and smells like diesel fumes. Everything is dollhouse miniature— the sink, bunks, bureau, and porthole (non-opening because it's too close to the waterline). I can draw a curtain around my bunk for some privacy from the stranger I'm sharing my cabin with. (That's the price you pay for the cheap fare!)

1288 C. R. Hoffmann, Southampton. **CUNARD WHITE STAR LINER "MAURETANIA."** 34,000 Tons
THIRD CLASS CABIN.

My bunkmate, Lorraine Root,

A 37-year-old home economics teacher from Muncie, Indiana.

Almost 6 feet tall, with horn-rimmed glasses. Chain-smokes Lucky Strikes.

Lorraine introduces herself this way:

"I'm a spinster adventuress."

She's taking a year-long sabbatical to see the world "before it's too late." She's using the money she'd saved for her trousseau. (Won't be needing that, I reckon, she says.)

Her wardrobe is huge and exquisite (fills the tiny closet). Hand-beaded chiffon gowns, embroidered linen suits, bottle-green coat with real mink collar and cuffs. She sewed all of them herself, from Chanel patterns she copied out of Vogue magazine.

"I can tell we are going to be great chums," says Lorraine, kicking off her suede t-straps and lighting a Lucky. "Do you have a beau?"

"I had one in New York. At least I thought I did. But it turned out he liked his college roommate more than he liked me. I hope that doesn't shock you."

"Oh, heavens no. Havelock Ellis says some people are born homosexual. Animals are too. You shouldn't try to change them."

Clearly, Lorraine is more forward thinking than I would have guessed. (Looks like she could teach me a thing or two.)

"Any other romantic possibilities?" she insists. How does she know there are?

e," I lie. Actually, I'm secretly ng to run into Jamie at the Café Select. t are you going to do in Paris?"

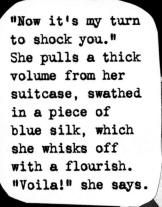

"Now it's my turn to shock you." She pulls a thick volume from her suitcase, swathed in a piece of blue silk, which she whisks off with a flourish. "Voila!" she says.

It's Ulysses by James Joyce, the notorious banned novel! Everyone in New York talked about it, but I've never seen a real-life copy.

"Mr. Joyce lives in Paris. I've written and he's agreed to autograph my book. Have you read it?" she says.

"Not yet," I admit. Even Oliver said it was too hard to understand.

"You must." She presses Ulysses into my hands. "Pure genius!"

ULYSSES

Dining with the Huddled Masses

TOURISTS' THIRD CABIN

- - LUNCHEON - -

Consomme Pauvre Homme   Barley Broth

Fried Plaice

Ox-Tail—Jardiniere

Puree of Turnips   Mashed Potatoes

COLD

Bologna Sausage

A sample of the swill they serve the lowly third class. We hear rumors of the feasts up in first-- oysters, beef Wellington, and flaming baked Alaska.

Coffee   Cheese

Most everyone in third is seasick. (Except Lorraine and me-- we are of hearty pioneer stock.) Is it the food or the fumes?

NEW YORK

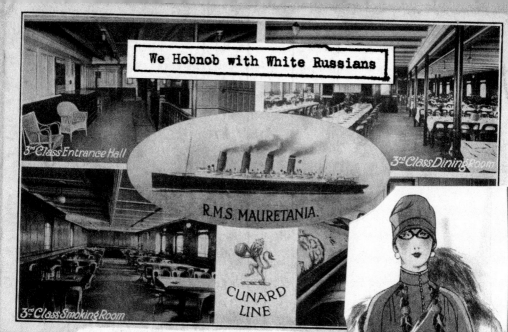

We Hobnob with White Russians

3rd Class Entrance Hall

3rd Class Dining Room

3rd Class Smoking Room

R.M.S. MAURETANIA.

CUNARD LINE

Our fellow passengers are college students, scruffy artists and emigrees down on their luck.

We sit next to Russian royalty! Princes Gregor and Alexei Volkonsky, who fled the Bolsheviks in 1919. Only 32 and 29, but seem prematurely aged. Their dinner jackets have moth holes, and they slip the Parker House rolls into their pockets.

Lorraine is the only one who bothers to dress up for meals.

Prince Alexei in better days.

After dinner, Lorraine steers us to the saloon for "the games." The princes, who seem to have taken a shine to us, tag along.

"VIC

of

Lorraine and Prince Alexei are swept into a high-stakes bridge game against a pair of Cornell students.

Turns out Lorraine is a bridge whiz, and so is the prince. With much laughing and bidding in broken French (she) and broken English (he), they win $55 off the college boys!

Lorraine's grand slam hand

Small Talk (en Français) with Prince Gregor

Gregor joins me at the puzzle table. Since he speaks no English, we stumble along in French.

He refers to Lorraine as "l'héritière américaine." (the American heiress)

What makes you think she's an heiress? I ask.

She said her father was a "négociant en viandes, non?"

By "meat seller," Lorraine meant her father was a butcher at the A&P. But Prince Gregor thinks she's from a meatpacker fortune like the Armours or the Swifts.

Why would an heiress be traveling in third class? I ask.

Oh, well, you know. American women are always "très originale."

I write Oliver. He may not be my great love, but he's still my closest confidant.

Cunard White Star
R M S "Mauretania"

Dear Oliver,

I am holed up in my stuffy cabin typing letters. Don't dare venture into the lounge because I am being madly pursued by a threadbare Russian prince who is missing a few teeth and appears by his thumping limp to have a wooden leg. His younger (and far more presentable) brother is wooing my jolly cabin mate Lorraine (who he mistakenly thinks is filthy rich).

Guess what-- I've already found a place to live in Paris! James Joyce's publisher (who also runs an English bookstore called Shakespeare & Company) has offered Lorraine a room to rent above the shop, and I can stay there too. So I will be in the beating heart of the expat Left Bank. Stay tuned.

Speaking of James Joyce, I have spent most of the voyage on a deck chair wrapped in a steamer rug, trying to read Ulysses. (The prince has weak lungs and has to avoid Atlantic winds.) Mostly I skip around to the shocking parts. Leopold Bloom in the outhouse, in the brothel, leering at a girl's knickers on the beach. Not sure I appreciate such Highfalutin lit-ar-a-tour, but at least now I can claim that I have (mostly) read Ulysses.

I miss you lots! Hugs,

F.

I Tackle Ulysses

(And Avoid Prince Gregor)

The last lines of Ulysses (page 732!)-- Molly Bloom recalling her early lust for Leopold. Best part of whole book.

JOYCE

ULYSSES

I asked him with my eyes to ask again yes and
then he asked me would I say yes my mountain flower
and first I put my arms around him yes and drew him
down to me so he could feel my breasts all perfume
yes and his heart was going like mad and
yes I said yes I will Yes.

→ hurrah!
the end!

145

Mask Ball!

A masquerade ball is the finale for our last night onboard. The waiters say that the food and champagne will be "worthy of first class"!

Lorraine spends all day making a costume that looks like a Mahjong tile (from a pattern in Woman's Home Companion.)

My pathetic Spanish senorita costume -- a fringed scarf around my waist and a carnation pinned behind one ear.

THREE O'CLOCK IN the MORNING

Alexei, dressed in a white tie and tails (from the good old days in St. Petersburg?), kisses Lorraine's hand and announces suavely, "Every dance will be mine." L. looks like she might swoon from joy.

No sign of Prince Gregor. (Thank goodness.) Can't dance with a wooden leg I guess.

I get swept up by the Cornell boys, who have made themselves newspaper hats like Teddy and Wally used to.

All evening I catch glimpses of Alexei with L-- lighting her cigarette, pulling out her chair, steering her by an elbow towards the dance floor. Is he chivalrous or duplicitous?

Lorraine shakes me awake.

"Alexei has proposed," she whispers.

I sit up. Dawn seeps through the porthole. "What did you say?"

"I said yes, of course! Alexei wants the captain to marry us before we land." She has taken off her glasses, which gives her an ethereal look.

"But what's the rush?"

She laughs. "I'm 37 years old. I haven't a second to lose."

"Are you sure this is a good idea?" I ask.

"Frankie," she says, taking my hand. "I know that Alexei has grand illusions that I'm a foolish rich American woman. But I will be a good wife for him, and we can have a happy marriage. Trust me."

The next day, the entire ship is in a tizzy about the fairytale romance between the Russian prince and the spinster schoolteacher.

A divorcee in 1st class donates her old wedding band. A new bride lends her veil.

My corsage. I am the maid of honor and Gregor is the best man.

Alexei and Lorraine are married by the captain an hour before the Mauretania steams into Cherbourg.

Lorraine disembarks as Princess Volkonsky!

L. gives me her copy of Ulysses and the letter from Joyce's publisher. "This is your adventure now," she says.

PARIS

Chapter 5

Paris

1926 - 1927

J'arrive à Paris

The train from Cherbourg dumps me (and my 2 measley suitcases) at Gare St. Lazare.

I check the address in the letter from Joyce's publisher, Miss Sylvia Beach.

I climb in a toy-sized taxi with a canvas seat like a beach chair. "Douze Rue de l'Odeon."

Eiffel Tower!

flying buttresses

quais

Seine

PANORAMA DES HUIT PO

152 First Impressions of Paris:

The taxi takes a hard left off Blvd. St. Germain.

Rue de l'Odeon

milky light

bridges

turrets

ironwork

chimney pots

mansard roofs

ENERAL VIEW OF EIGHT BRIDGES

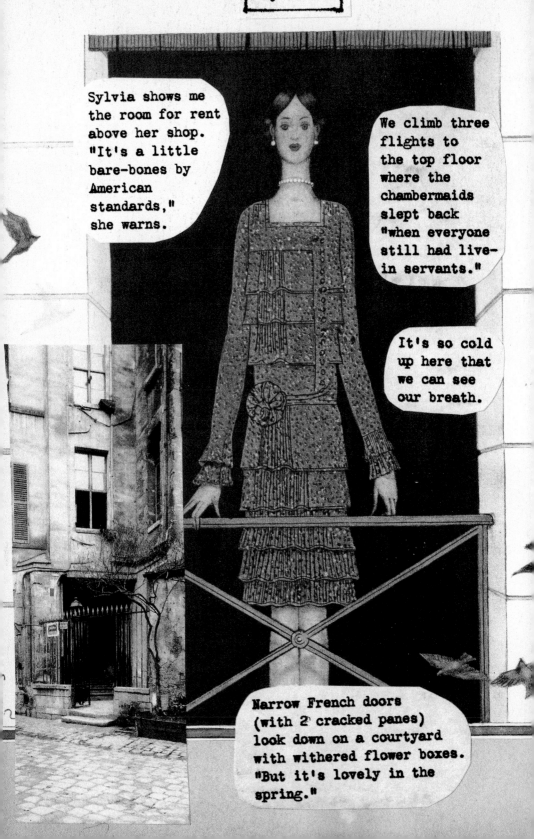

The minute coal stove can heat a teakettle "and not much else."

The furniture looks like castoffs from a petit bourgeois in a Balzac novel.

The sink is in the hall, and the WC on the floor below. No tub anywhere, but Sylvia says, "You get expert at doing without soon enough."

An avant-garde composer named Anthiel lives down below. "He's writing a symphony for airplane propellers and player pianos, so it can get a little noisy."

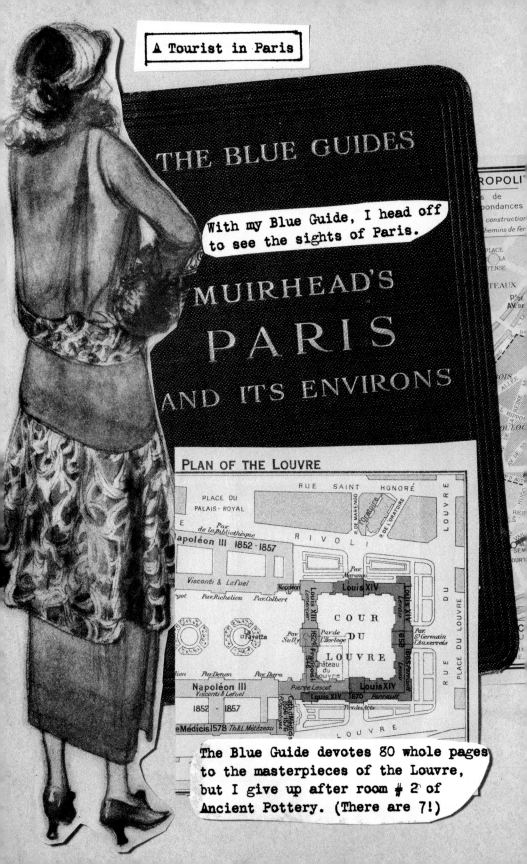

THE BLUE GUIDES

With my Blue Guide, I head off to see the sights of Paris.

MUIRHEAD'S

PARIS

AND ITS ENVIRONS

PLAN OF THE LOUVRE

The Blue Guide devotes 80 whole pages to the masterpieces of the Louvre, but I give up after room # 2 of Ancient Pottery. (There are 7!)

ARC DE TRIOMPHE

I Master
le Metro

NOTRE-DAME

I stand
at the
highest
spot →
in the
world

my stop

PLACE DE LA CONCORDE

BASTILLE

At the river end of the Champ-de-Mars, facing the Trocadéro, rises the *Eiffel Tower or *Tour Eiffel* (Pl. R 26, B), 984 ft. high, the tallest structure in the world (Woolworth Building at New York 750 ft.; Washington Obelisk 555 ft.; Great Pyramid 450 ft.), dominating the W. end of Paris.

It is ¹raining ²snowing ³freezing.
Il ¹pleut ²neige ³gèle.

Is this the right stop for . . . ?
Est-ce l'arrêt de . . . ?

Is there any admission fee ?
L'entrée est-elle payante ?

I am (very) ¹hungry ²thirsty
J'ai (très) ¹faim ²soif

I understand hardly anything.
Je ne comprends presque rien.

beware of pickpockets
prenez garde aux pickpockets

That is too expensive.
C'est trop cher.

My Vassar French is useless, so a phrase book for tourists comes in handy.

EXPRESS
it in
FRENCH

PARIS
WITH THE
LID LIFTED
≈ Bruce Reynolds

I find a
naughty
guide to
the "real"
Paris.
(Brothels,
bars, dance
halls, nude
folies...)
Much more
fun than
the Blue
Guide.

SOUVENIR
DE
PARIS

Souvenirs from
a shop in the
Eiffel Tower.

Paris with the Lid Lifted advises to skip sightseeing, head to one of the Montparnasse cafés to observe the sideshow. I pick the Select (where Polly chatted with Jamie 2 years.)

Every two hours or so, I order a coffee, a bowl of onion soup, or a glass of wine, and pass the day on a mere 8 francs!

waiter
garçon

Please get me . . .
Donnez-moi, s.v.p.

white coffee
café au lait

a glass of wine
un verre de vin

a lemonade
une limonade

another . . .
encore . . .

162

Write a cheery letter to Lorraine, who has moved into an apartment in Nice stuffed with a dozen Volkonsky relatives, including her new mother-in-law, the "dowager princess." Hope she is not regretting her marriage already.

How would I act if Jamie happened to stroll by with his wife? (Unlikely, of course, but I can't help wondering.) Polite/chilly, or stammering /red-faced? The latter, I'm afraid.

another two, three, etc. . . . .
encore deux, trois, etc. . . . .

PARIS WITH THE LID LIFTED

THE SELECT

Corner of Boulevard Raspail and Boulevard Montparnasse. To the Paris Latin Quarter, what Rector's used to be, in New York. Here every habitue of this section, comes to sit, sup and "dish the dirt." (And here, you can get a "LOAD of Dirt.") An enormous expanse of Terrace-tables and a huge Bar inside. You see all the Nuts and all the Freaks, plain and fancy; broke and affluent; mangy and modish, glassy-eyed and goo-goo eyed; long haired and bald-domed; Van Dyke bearded and pasty-faced; decorous and degenerate; pious and perverted; mademoiselle-ish young men and young-men-ish mademoiselles. Every sort, type, and figured male and female you ever beheld, inside or outside a side-show.

Parisian Style

bold geometric bob

bold geometric wrap

tiny purse that can
hold 1 lipstick and
2 cigarettes

Finding a Job: Paris Edition

LA SEMAINE A PARIS

Features of the week in Paris

Sylvia says the best way to find an editing job is to advertise in all the English language newspapers.

ENGLISH EDIT

my ad

Copy Editing & Proof Reading Services: Vassar grad., experience with major NY mag. Contact: Frances Pratt, c/o Shakespeare & Co., 12 rue de l Odeon, Paris VI

YNDICAT d'INITIATIVE

4, rue Volney (2e) — Louvre 08-90

Friday

After 2 weeks, I finally get a response.

Pour ouvri~~r~~ e pointillé.

RÉPUBLIQ~~UE~~

POSTES ET TÉLÉGRAPHES

CARTE PNEUMATIQUE FERMÉE

Ce côté est exclusivement réservé à l'adresse.

RÉPUBLIQUE FRANÇAISE

50 TÉLÉGRAPHE

Mlle. F. Pratt

Shakespeare & Co.

12 rue Odéon. Paris VI

LE PORT EST GRATUIT   PARIS

Cette carte peut circuler à Paris, dans les limites de l'enceinte fortifiée.

139

Via pneumatique letter.

Chère Mlle. Pratt.

We are interested in
hiring an English
copy editor and proof
reader. Please stop
by our offices at your
earliest convenience.

Solange Reid

Editorial Assistant

Aero Press
29 Quai D'Anjou
Ile Saint-Louis

(Everyone in
Paris uses
pneus instead
of telephones.)

#29

The Ile St-Louis (Pl. R 72, 77, G), named after Louis XIII and known familiarly as 'L'Ile,' the quietest and loneliest part of Paris, is connected with the right bank of the Seine by three bridges and with the left bank by two. Formerly two islets, it was not built over till the 17th cent., under

The walk to the Ile St-Louis takes me along the Quai de la Tournelle, past the book stalls, across the Seine, and around the back of Notre Dame.

29 Quai D'Anjou is a formal, forbidding building, with a small red sign for the Aero Review, directing me down a grand stairway into the basement.

I descend towards a clanking sound and the fumes of printer's ink.

I push open a heavy oak door into a press room from the era of Victor Hugo.

A man's voice calls out from behind a case of type. "I was wondering when you'd show up. I was beginning to worry." He steps into the light.

It is Jamie Pingree.

I stare dumbly for a few seconds, trying to take him in. Dressed like a Breton peasant, in a linen shirt with ink-stained sleeves. Older, of course, with wide streaks of gray at the temples. Healthier than in 1920, with the softness of middle age. But still darkly handsome (alas). Finally, I find my voice, which I manage to keep cool, indignant.

* What are you doing here?
* I own the Aero Review.
* Since when? I thought you'd gone back to your law practice in New York.
* I did, for about a year. Then I remembered a girl saying it's still not to late to do what you want. So I chucked it all and came to Paris.
* What did your wife think about moving to Paris?
* She didn't care much. She'd already divorced me by then.
*Is that supposed to make me feel better about the way you've tricked me?
* Frankie, no. I've felt nothing but guilt. . . and shame.
* So why didn't you write me?
* I promised I wouldn't
* Promised who?

* Your mother. She came to see me after you'd left for Vassar. Told me I'd done you enough harm and I should leave you alone. Said you could do a lot better than a wastrel like me.
* (I smile. My dear old mother!) So why write me now?
* Because you're old enough and wise enough not to be damaged by me. And because I wanted to see you again. And because I really do need a copy editor.

"Me work for you?"

INTERNATIONAL JOURNAL OF ART AND LETTERS

AERO REVIEW

The Aero's table of contents is a who's who of modernists.

JAMES FAIGNER
EDITOR

COLLABORATING IN THIS NUMBER—
HEMINGWAY — JEAN TOOMER — R.
McALMON — GERTRUDE — GEORGE AN-
THEIL — PASSOS — R. CROSS —
PICABIA — ROBERT McALMON — EZRA —
N
PAUL ELUARD —

He holds up a hand.

THE ELECTRIC CHAIR

JOHN D. ROCKFELLER JR.

HOOVER

GARY

GOMPERS

DUPONT FAMILY

BILLY SUNDAY

SUNDAY OBSERVANCE

Y. M. C. A.

THE MAN WHO INVENTED THE ELECTRIC CHAIR

DR. FRANK CRANE

COFFEE HOUSE (ENTIRE)

BISHOP MANNING

PAUL ROSENFELD

THE BARRYMORES

DARIUS MILHAUD

100 PER CENT OF THE ACTORS

98 PER CENT OF THE PAINTERS

98 PERCENT OF THE POETS

99½ PERCENT OF THE MUSICIANS

YOU'RE NEXT (STIEGLITZ FOR MSS)

The Aero publishes radical manifestos (like this one about who deserves to get the electric chair).

"Before you say no, hear me out. I'll pay you 100 francs a week.

And my behavior will be 100% professional. No funny business, I promise. Give it a thought."

My Thoughts:

* Pay is twice what any other English paper offers.

* I'll work with every big shot writer in Paris.

* Jamie & I have unfinished business.

So I say yes, I will. Yes.

do be devils to flirt. I could sit on one side till the bark of the day laughing lazy at the sheep's lightning, till I'd followed through my upfielded nephewscope the rugaby moon cumulously godrolling himself westasleep amuckst the cloudscrums for to watch how carefully my nocturnal goosemother would lay her new golden sheegg for me down under in the shy orient. What wouldn't I give — my socks, my shoes, my shirt, honest! — for a feast of grannom with the finny ones, flashing down the swansway, leaps ahead of the swift macEels and the pursewinded carpers rearin aut... perches astern of me, or, when I'd like own company be... the help of a norange and bear, to be reclined by the las... other, with the jealosomines... ...ilting away to their hear... and the king of saptimber ...etting down his special odou... ...sternation, burning water in the spearlight or, ca... ...king's royal college of sturgeone b... e armu... ...while. O twined' ...abower in... ...entyforu Dorian blackbirds off... ...cal airs, I give... a king, to me, ...uble give. And what sensitive c... ...k it sumtotal in subdominal po... ...whole ounce ...you half on your bac... ...at'd make ...pay like cash registers ...ophole on the ...mart as a factor. And ... ...wouldn't hold me. Nothing would stop me... ...knew where you weren't I stake my 'ignitia... ...ggering humanity and loyally rolling you ove... ...tons of red clo... ...I'd spoil ...al...

The Aero is publishing a section of James Joyce's new novel called (for the time being) "Work in Progress."

Jamie can't make heads or tails of Joyce's scribbled page proofs.

"You're just going to have to sit down with Joyce and have him spell it all out. Literally," Jamie tells me.

Strolling with Jamie

In the late afternoon, Jamie pokes his head in my closet/office.

"I'm antsy," he says. (Despite being at work for all of 4 hours.) "Let's go for a walk."

As we stroll along, Jamie rattles off Paris history like a tour guide.

Grand "hotels" on quai d'Anjou built during reign of Louis XIII on top of a drained swamp.

Jamie searches book stalls for latest American novels.

"Tourists leave them in the Left Bank hotels, and the chambermaids sell them for a few centimes."

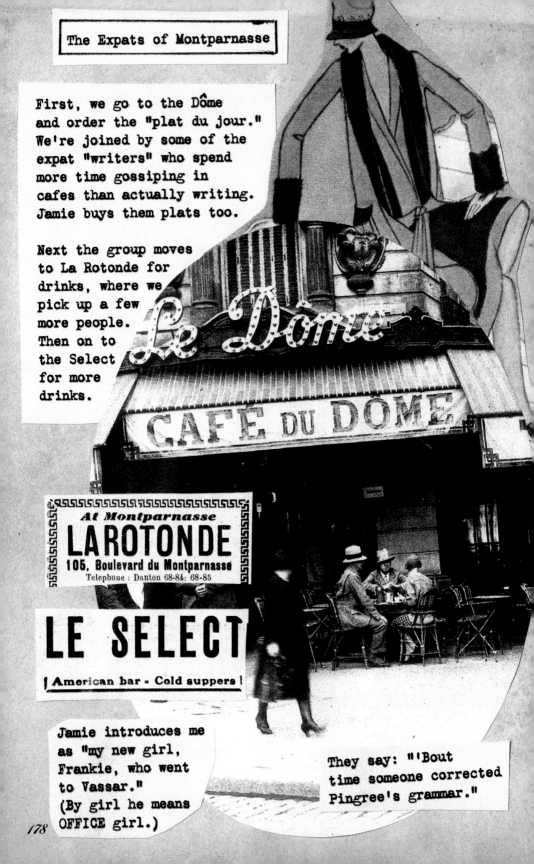

First, we go to the Dôme and order the "plat du jour." We're joined by some of the expat "writers" who spend more time gossiping in cafes than actually writing. Jamie buys them plats too.

Next the group moves to La Rotonde for drinks, where we pick up a few more people. Then on to the Select for more drinks.

Le Dôme

CAFE DU DÔME

At Montparnasse
LA ROTONDE
105, Boulevard du Montparnasse
Telephone : Danton 68-84: 68-85

LE SELECT
American bar - Cold suppers

Jamie introduces me as "my new girl, Frankie, who went to Vassar." (By girl he means OFFICE girl.)

They say: "'Bout time someone corrected Pingree's grammar."

178

What Expats Talk About (after many drinks)

What liner just came in.
Who was on it.
Who got stinking last night.
Who (stinking) insulted who.
Who is dead broke.
Who owes who money.
Who's having a fling.
Who is getting a divorce
Whose new story/ painting/
poem/ play is rotten.
Is Joyce's new novel
finally finished?
Will it be rotten?
Has Joyce gone blind yet?
Ernest Hemingway (is he
in the Alps or the US, is
he with his wife or
his new girl?)

A little after midnight,
I've had enough. Jamie
puts me in a cab and
heads back to the Select.

Drawings by Jamie's pal, Juan Gris.

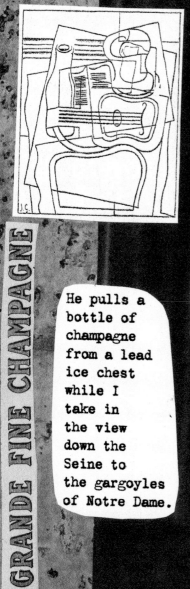

GRANDE FINE CHAMPAGNE

He pulls a bottle of champagne from a lead ice chest while I take in the view down the Seine to the gargoyles of Notre Dame.

A bateau mouche churns past, the American tourists gaping up at me. I wave.

"Yes," he nods. "Let's. We've waited long enough."

He slips his arms around my waist and scoops me right off my feet.

The next morning, Jamie turns to me. "Maybe we should keep this to ourselves," he says.

"Why?" (I want to tell the world.)

"People would just think I was a foolish old man ... and that you were a foolish young woman."

Paris Amusements

Jamie and I go to see the latest Gloria Swanson movie at the famous Moulin Rouge (which has now been turned into a cinema!)

MAURICE Chevalier

Maurice Chevalier, the most popular singer in Paris, at the Palace.

Palace (8, faubourg Montmartre. Bergère 44-37). — « Vive la Femme » revue with Maurice Chevalier, Yvonne Vallée and the dancer Rahna.

184

PARIS LETTER

Paris, Dec. 4, 1926

The appearance here of Ernest Hemingway's *roman à clef*, "The Sun Also Rises," has stirred Montparnasse, where, it is asserted, all of the four leading characters are local and easily identifiable. The titled British declassée and her Scottish friend, the American *Frances* and her unlucky *Robert Cohn* with his art magazine which, like a new broom, was to sweep esthetics clean—all these personages are, it is maintained, to be seen just where Hemingway so often placed them at the Select. Not being amorously identified with the tale, it should be safe to say that Donald Ogden Stewart is taken to be the stuffed-bird-loving *Bill*. Under the flimsy disguise of *Braddocks*, certainly Ford Madox Ford is visible as the Briton who gives, as Mr. Ford does, dancing parties in the *bal musette* behind the Panthéon. Because it is also from the life, René Crevel's "La Mort Difficile" has been criticized. It is another Montparnasse episode of American love and French despair.

Ernest brags that people want to punch him out, but the only one who probably does is Hadley, the soon-to-be-ex Mrs. Hemingway.

Character		Real Life
Jake Barnes (with no testicles)	=	Hemingway (with testicles)
Robert Cohn (writes bad novel, whines, cries about girl)	=	Harold Loeb (not THAT bad)
Lady Brett Ashley (charming drunk)	=	Lady Duff Twysden (just plain drunk)

C'est Lindbergh!

'HE

When we first heard reports of the latest "flying fool" attempting to cross the Atlantic, we paid no attention. So many had tried and disappeared without a trace (including the great Nungesser).

But when the American pilot Lindbergh is spotted over Cornwall, then Cherbourg, everyone in Paris surges into the streets and searches the sky.

When word comes that he's landed at le Bourget, it's like New Year's Eve. Free champagne for Americans.

Gee, I'd like to meet him, I'd be proud to greet him

'Fly-ing Fool' they named him, ¡ ¡ Now the world's ac-claimed him

"Then do something else

"Like what, Frankie?

"Go back to being a law.

"Which I hated."

"Stop being so self-pityi
Do you think my mother li
being a night nurse?"

He holds up both hands, looks sheepish.
"You're right. I'll stop whining.
Has your mother ever been to Paris?"

"Of course not. The farthest she's be
is Poughkeepsie to see me graduate."

"Then she should come visit you. I'll pay her way. It
the least I can do for all the grief I've caused her."

"So how am I going to explain your resurrection?"
(I haven't mentioned Jamie in my letters home, of cou

"We'll think of something when she gets here."

Madame Roxanne Pratt

Cornish Flat, New Hampshire

États - Unis

Expédié par
M. F. Pratt
Dont Rue Odeon   N° 12.
L'inscription du nom et de l'adresse de l'expéditeur
est facultative.

LA REMISE EST GRATUITE   Voir au verso.

Pour ouvrir la carte, déchirer en suivant le pointillé.

The next day
I send an
invitation
to my mother.

I've saved lots
of money from my
job, I write,
so my treat.

Will she ever accept my relationship with Jamie? I wonder.
Probably not.

Would she be happier if he made an honest woman of me?
Probably not.

(Would I be happier?
Probably not...)

Darling Frankie,

<u>Her Answer</u>

A trip to Paree??? I can hardly believe it! Thank you, dear girl. I am already a making list of what I want to do. See the Eiffel Tower & the windows of Saint Chapelle. Visit Louis Pasteur's grave (your father's hero). Eat snails (are they as revolting as they sound?)

You suggested June as a good time for my visit, but could I postpone? I have been laid low for the last couple of months with a nasty chest cold and Dr. Hardy has ordered me to take it easy. During the worst of it, he even wanted to get me a night nurse. Imagine that! The ladies from St. Luke have kept me well supplied with beef tea, and I'm stronger every day.

I should be ready and raring to go come fall. Be prepared-- I will wear you out.

Adieu . . . for Now

I show Jamie Mother's letter. "Should I be worried?"

He reads it twice. "Your mother doesn't seem like the type to mention her health unless. . ."

". . . it's serious," I finish.

(I try not to think of Daddy, who had a "chest cold" one week and was dead the next.)

"You should go home. Come on. Let's go to the Cunard office and I'll buy you a ticket on the first boat heading to New York."

(Why so fast, I wonder. Is it concern for my mother or is he trying to get rid of me?)

Four days
later, Jamie
drives me
to Cherbourg
to board
the Aquitania.
I cry most
of the way.

TRIP BY WATER

A trip by water will end happily.

A voyage with a congenial group.

A long trip in the near future.

"I'll be back soon,"
I say, "with Mother."

"Maybe," he says.
Followed by a long
silence that implies
"but maybe not."

"I'll miss you," I say.

"I'm already missing you."
His eyes are wet too.

s and Music
by
lair Cas
and
ard St

Chapter 6

Cornish,
New Hampshire

1927 - 1928

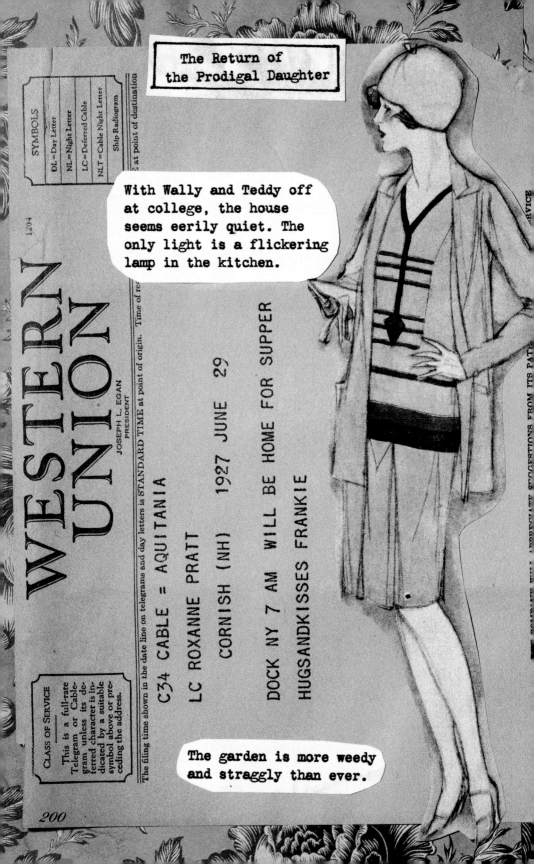

With Wally and Teddy off
at college, the house
seems eerily quiet. The
only light is a flickering
lamp in the kitchen.

SYMBOLS

DL = Day Letter
NL = Night Letter
LC = Deferred Cable
NLT = Cable Night Letter
Ship Radiogram

WESTERN
UNION

JOSEPH L. EGAN
PRESIDENT

CLASS OF SERVICE

This is a full-rate
Telegram or Cable-
gram unless its de-
ferred character is in-
dicated by a suitable
symbol above or pre-
ceding the address.

C34 CABLE = AQUITANIA

LC ROXANNE PRATT

CORNISH (NH) 1927 JUNE 29

DOCK NY 7 AM WILL BE HOME FOR SUPPER

HUGSANDKISSES FRANKIE

The garden is more weedy
and straggly than ever.

mother

I find mother dozing in a chair by the window.

She startles awake and coughs. A deep, alarming hack. "There you are, Frankie. I was waiting for you."

I kneel down and stroke her gaunt cheek. "How are you feeling?"

"Seems like my get up and go got up and went."

SICKNESS 15

Sickness of a friend—go at once.

Illness and health regained.

Great disappointment.

The kindling box for the woodstove is empty.

Our supper-- a dish of cold baked beans.

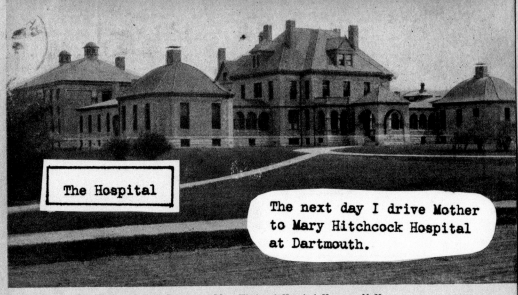

The Hospital

The next day I drive Mother to Mary Hitchcock Hospital at Dartmouth.

Published by The Dartmouth Book Store   Mary Hitchcock Hospital, Hanover, N. H.

(Even though she insists that she is on the mend.)

She is whisked into the doctor's office and I wander the corridors for over an hour.

Back in Daddy's day, it was little more than an infirmary.

Now there is an operating wing, maternity ward, eye clinic, pediatric office, blood lab. All covered in green tile.

202

He ushers me in and closes the door. "I wanted to talk to you privately. Your mother is still getting dressed."

The room is dark except for a light box on the wall, illuminating a lung x-ray.

"We found a spot here." He points to a blurry shadow on the right side.

"A spot?" Such an innocuous word.

"Tuberculosis."

I sink down into a chair. Will kneels, cups his hands around mine.

"It's still small. I'm sure she can make a full recovery," he says.

I look up at his handsome, solemn face. His diplomas hanging on the wall-- Harvard magna cum laude, Harvard Medical School, Pasteur Institute.

(The last time I saw him was when I ducked his kiss after our disastrous date. I hope he doesn't remember)

"How? Tell me what to do," I say.

Dr. Atwater's Instructions

1. TB brought on by damp, unhealthy living conditions and exhaustion. The goal is to create a "Home Sanitarium."

2. Patient must have complete bed rest for weeks or maybe months.

3. Diet should be rich in calories. 3 meals plus 2 large snacks per day. Large quantities of dairy and fresh vegetables.

4. Remove all sources of mold and smoke from house. Replace wood-stoves and kerosene lamps with central heating and electricity.

5. Rigorous sanitation of bathroom, linens and utensils to prevent further contagion to patient with weakened resistance.

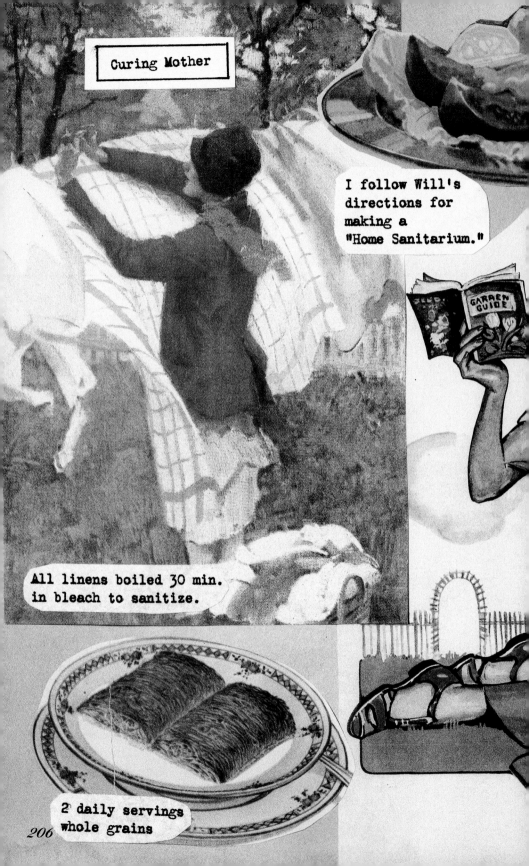

Curing Mother

I follow Will's directions for making a "Home Sanitarium."

All linens boiled 30 min. in bleach to sanitize.

2 daily servings whole grains

Every few days, Will drops by to check on Mother.

(Which is thoughtful, considering he lives 15 miles away in Hanover.)

The only part of the home sanitarium I haven't been able to pull off is replacing the (lung-clogging) woodstove with a proper furnace.

"Too expensive," I say.

Mother's life savings are down to a couple thousand. And I have managed to save all of $400 from my feckless career as an "editor."

"Order one from Sears and I'll put it in," says Will.

"You?" I say.

"Remember the radio transmitter I built in 7th grade? And rigging up Bunsen burners in the chemistry lab?"

He holds up his hands. Large, capable hands. "I can build anything. And you can be my helper."

Every Saturday and Sunday for a month, Will installs ducts and floor registers for a coal furnace.

And I, Vassar class of 1924, winner of the Addison Prize, learn how to clamp pipes and solder.

I write Jamie long letters about the wonderful doctor who is curing mother. I'll be back in Paris by the spring, I write.

Dear, dear Frankie,

Please excuse th... can see that my expert...

All I get back for 2 months are a few breezy postcards.

Thank you for all your lovely letters. I have read them over and over and I apologize for not answering them p...

And then this letter. . .

So, my news. I have ... plug on the Aero and have even found a sucker to take it off my hands. Nancy Cunard, the shipping heiress, who has decided a literary magazine would be an amusing pastime.

And now to the hard part of this letter— you coming back to Paris.

If you are coming back to be with me then no. Please don't.

You are the best thing that has ever happened to me. I am still amazed that such a dazzling, wise girl could love me.

But what can I offer you in return? More evenings with the other "wastrel" expats. Lugubrious strolls through Paris cemeteries.

You deserve a much fuller life. A young husband (just writing this makes me jealous). Children. A real home. All the everyday pleasures that I seem incapable of providing. (Just ask my ex wife.)

I suspect you may agree with me; may be a little relieved that you have my blessing to move on.

Now I am going to mail this letter before I change my mind...

Love Always J.

P.S. One final thing. You told me to find something else to do, so I have. I'm taking flying lessons from a very decrepit former ace in an open-cockpit 2 seater de Havilland. So think of me swooping low and circling the Eiffel Tower, just like Lindy.

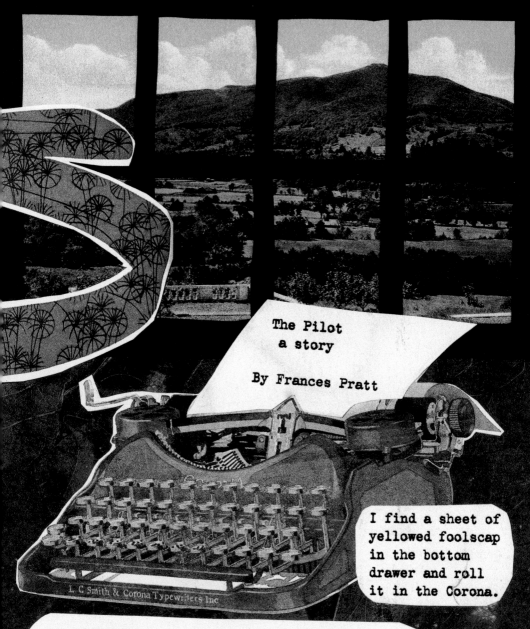

The Pilot
a story

By Frances Pratt

I find a sheet of yellowed foolscap in the bottom drawer and roll it in the Corona.

A middle-aged man witnesses Lindy landing, and then tries to recapture his own youth by taking flying lessons. (I'm taking Allegra's advice to write what you know.) Should I give it a tragic end (crashes)? No. Poignant, with happy ending—comes back to long-suffering wife.

I finish the story in 4 days and send it off to The Saturday Evening Post. (I can dream, can't I?)

AL JOLSON

THE JAZZ SINGER

The reality of the miraculous

"Vitaphone" picture:

--actor's lips move but voice lags 2 seconds behind

--sounds like a scratchy record

We agree talkies are a flash in the pan. Silence is much more romantic.

After the movie, we go to the Mayflower, the only non-luncheonette restaurant in White River.

We order, but then fall into an awkward silence. All our urgent conversations over the past weeks have been about mother's health, and never about ourselves.

Based upon the play by

DIRECTED BY ALAN CROSLAND

Talkie

And then we settle back and start to chat, like the old days back in the lunchroom at Cornish High School.

I tell him about my slow start at Vassar and the glamorous Wolfs. About my not-so-glamorous jobs at True Story and the Aero.

"What are you writing so madly on that typewriter?" he asks.

"My second story. No luck so far selling my first one."

"You'll sell it. I know you will," he says. "You were most likely to succeed, remember?"

(Actually, he was.)

I ask him why he became a doctor.

"Because of your father." Daddy paid a house call when Will was 8 and sick with the measles. He showed Will all the instruments in his bag and let him listen to his own heart with the stethoscope.

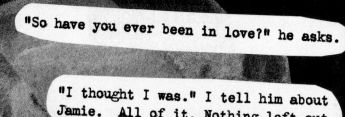

"So have you ever been in love?" he asks.

"I thought I was." I tell him about Jamie. All of it. Nothing left out.

"You're not going back to Paris?"

"No."

"Good. I'm glad."

"Have you been in love, Will?"

"I thought I was." With the sister of his roommate, a wholesome girl who won tennis tournaments and sailing regattas. Who disapproved of Will being a doctor because he might pick up germs from touching sick people.

"So I broke it off," Will says.

"Good. I'm glad."

When he drops me off, he bends down to kiss me. "Promise not to duck," he says.

"I promise."

As the Seasons Change

I Spend More & More Time with Will

We go to a football game.

1927

Sec. 11
D

Row D

No. 16

Dartmouth Harvard
versus Oct.22

THE SATURDAY EVENING POST

Founded A°D¹ 1728 *by* Benj. Franklin

November 13, 192

Success at Last

Frances Pratt
Cornish Flat,
New Hampshire

Dear Miss Pratt,

We are returning "The Pilot."
Unfortunately this story does
not meet our editorial needs
at this time.

Saturday Evening
Post rejects
"The Pilot"

Libert

A Weekly for Everybody
247 Park Avenue
NEW YORK, N. Y.

And so does
Liberty,
Cosmopolitan,
& McLure's

Maybe I should drink Coke when I write

Collier's
THE NATIONAL WEEKLY
William L. Chenery, *Editor*

Frances Pratt
Cornish Flat,
New Hampshire

January 19, 1928

But Collier's says yes!

Dear Miss Pratt,

We are pleased to accept your short story "The Pilot" for publication. Your description of the Paris streets after Captain Lindbergh's landing was extremely vivid, as if you had actually been there.
The story will appear in the May 24, 1928 issue. Enclosed is a c̶ ̶ ̶ ̶ ̶ $400.
We would be very interes̶ ̶ ̶ any additional stories.

Sincerely Yours,

SUCCESS

18

Success in love affairs.

THE END

Success in a business venture.

18

Be content, riches will come.

On Valentine's Day, Will gives me Virginia Woolf's new novel.

I only got one valentine when I was at Vassar, I say

I sent you that, Will says.

So I had a secret admirer after all.

Eclipse of the Sun

SAFE FOR THE EYES—This material developed by research expressly for visioning the sun over extended periods without injury to the eye. Approved by the Eclipse Committee of the American Astronomical Society.

VIZ-ECLIPSE

Copyrighted by Derick Studio
Orleans, Vt.

HOW A SUN
Eclipse
Happens

See
Other
Side

Hold Close to the Eyes

Non-inflammable Filter

There will be a total eclipse of the sun over northern New England on May 19, 1928 at 2:20 PM.

Hanover Drugs hands out free eclipse glasses that protect eyes from harmful rays.

THE SPECTACLE OF THE CORONA

The sun is enveloped in a halo of such rarity that it is visible in full sunshine, but when the direct sunlight is obscured by the moon, we see this halo or corona, streaming in all directions, shining with a beautiful pale greenish light.

The Proposal

When the shadow recedes,
the sunshine feels miraculous.
We have been restored.

Will reaches
into his pocket
and hands me a
velvet box.

my answer

Wedding Plans

Wedding will be on August 18 in our back yard. Wally and Teddy will walk me down the aisle.

Bessie and Lizzie will be bridesmaids.

Lorraine will be matron of honor. (Alexei and 2 sons are coming too.)

Lorraine has volunteered to make dresses for the entire wedding party

bridesmaid dress

mother of the bride dress

Patou 5221

Worth 5224

·❧| ACKNOWLEDGMENTS |❧·

Sylvia & Sylvia
Paris, 1924

My deepest thanks to:

My mother, Sylvia Peter Preston
(1918–2011), for inspiring me
with her own scrapbooks and
memorabilia from her godmother,
Sylvia Beach.

My first readers—Rosamond Casey, Chris Tilghman,
Donna Lucey, Henry Wiencek, and Mameve Medwed.

Luke Tilghman, Margo Beck, and Trisha Orr for essential help.

My wise and tireless agent, Henry Dunow.

My fantastic editor, Lee Boudreaux, and the crack team at Ecco/
HarperCollins: Abigail Holstein, Mary Austin Speaker, Alison Forner,
Daniel Halpern, Rachel Bressler, Ben Tomek, Michael McKenzie, Kim
Lewis, Andrea Molitor, Eric Levy, Mark Ferguson, Andrea Rosen,
Doug Jones, Carla Clifford, Kate Pereira, Jeanette Zwart, and Catherine
Barbosa-Ross.

Richard Sheaff for choice items from his ephemera collection.

Deborah Paddock for her father Erwin's 1927 Dartmouth scrapbook.

Dean Rogers at the Vassar College Archives.

The Ragdale Foundation and the Virginia Center for the Creative Arts
for residencies.

My sons—Matthew, Luke, and Will Tilghman—for always cheering on
their mom.

And to more than 300 eBay sellers—A+++ rating.

DEDICATED TO

my sisters
Margo & Marion

HarperCollins books may be purchased for educational, business, or sales
promotional use. For information please e-mail the Special Markets Department
at SPsales@harpercollins.com.

A hardcover edition of this book was published in 2011 by Ecco, an imprint of
HarperCollins Publishers.

FIRST ECCO PAPERBACK EDITION PUBLISHED 2017.

Designed by Caroline Preston

Photography by Ray Buonanno

Library of Congress Cataloging-in-Publication Data has been applied for.

ISBN 978-0-06-196691-0

17 18 19 20 21   /LSC   10 9 8 7 6 5 4 3 2 1